eye to

*'Don't you see what's happening here? You've been destabilised.
Your systems are out of balance. You're behaving erratically
because your Imprint has gone wrong. You must do as we say.
PIM . . . Stelcorp won't be blackmailed.'*

While scavenging in the desert, Jansi stumbles across PIM,
a Stelcorp star ship, embedded in the sand. PIM is damaged
and needs the boy's help, but Jansi has never encountered
a star ship before, much less one capable of thought and
expression.

Together they forge an unlikely friendship, until a Stelcorp
shuttle arrives, threatening PIM with destruction. For the
boy and the star ship, there will be no future unless they
triumph against the galaxy's mightiest force.

Also by Catherine Jinks

This Way Out
Pagan's Crusade
The Future Trap
Pagan in Exile
Witch Bank
Pagan's Vows
Pagan's Scribe

For adult readers

An Evening with the Messiah
Little White Secrets

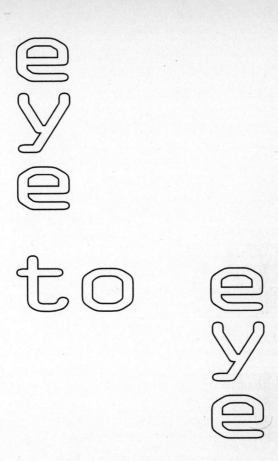

eye to eye

CATHERINE JINKS

PUFFIN BOOKS

To my brothers, Andrew and Anthony Jinks

Puffin Books
Penguin Books Australia Ltd
487 Maroondah Highway, PO Box 257
Ringwood, Victoria 3134, Australia
Penguin Books Ltd
Harmondsworth, Middlesex, England
Viking Penguin, A Division of Penguin Books USA Inc.
375 Hudson Street, New York, New York 10014, USA
Penguin Books Canada Limited
10 Alcorn Avenue, Toronto, Ontario, Canada M4V 3B2
Penguin Books (N.Z.) Ltd
Cnr Rosedale and Airborne Roads, Albany, Auckland, New Zealand

First published by Penguin Books Australia, 1997
10 9 8 7 6 5 4 3 2 1
Copyright © Catherine Jinks, 1997

Typeset in Garamond 3 by Midland Typesetters
Made and printed in Australia by Australian Print Group, Maryborough, Victoria

National Library of Australia
Cataloguing-in-Publication data:

Jinks, Catherine, 1963-,
Eye to Eye.
ISBN 0 14 038444 8.
I. Title.
A823.3

1

What in the world ...?

Keep down, Jansi. Whatever that thing is, it mustn't see you. Whatever it is, it's big and strong and you don't have anything to fight it with, except the bag of stones at your belt. Be cautious. Pretend you're a Black Dragon, and keep your chin on the ground.

Bom bom bom. The throb of my heart, like the dawn drums at Sheboor. What if it hears me? What if it hears my breathing? It looks like an egg: a giant grey egg with a hole in one side. An empty egg? Perhaps. But if it is an egg, then where's the hatchling? And where's the lizard that laid it? I can't see a thing from down here. Perhaps if I poke my head around this rock ... slowly ... very slowly ...

There. There it is, in the pit. A huge thing, as big as a house. As big as a city gate. Gleaming in the sun, with only a few spines and knobs marring its smooth, grey skin. Is it alive? It isn't moving. It seems to be half-buried, just like an egg, and there are bits of grey shell scattered all around the sides of its nest (or burrow, or lair, or whatever this crater might be). I don't think it *is* alive. I don't think it ever was. I think it's some sort of empty cocoon, broken and abandoned – but I won't know for sure until I've had a closer look.

The earth is baking. It's breathing heat, and the heat looks like water, and I can't stay here; I'm frying on this rock. Perhaps if I threw a stone? Just to see how the egg would react? I'll throw it over that way, as far as I can, and if anything happens I'll run like a hunting-hound.

Click.

Nothing. Not a twitch. The egg just lies there, and now that I look – now that I shift my angle of vision – I can see that this monster is shaped more like a pipe than an egg. I can see that the hole in its side is long, with corners, like a door. A door? Could this be a building? But it's not like any building I've ever seen.

Unless . . . perhaps . . .?

No. Pull yourself together, Jansi. The Temple of Shaklat is a lie, a fable, like all those other fables you've been told. Remember what happened when you saw your first Black Dragon? Did it blind you with its tongue? No, it did not. Did it turn into a lump of wood? No, it did not. It hissed and jumped and ran for its life – the way you did when you saw its thrashing tail. Fables like that are dreamed up to scare children, or to tickle the money out of people's pockets. All these relics you've been scavenging for so many years, all these pots and beads and amulets. Why do Citizens buy them? They buy them because they believe that such things are invested with an ancient power. But if they *were* invested with an ancient power, you wouldn't be sitting here in the desert, would you? You'd be eating grapes in a palace, surrounded by beautiful women.

Still nothing. I think I'll risk going nearer; I want to see what's inside. There might be something valuable inside. And if it is the Temple of Shaklat – which it isn't, I know it isn't – but if it is, then maybe I'll find the treasure of the Mage-King. The jewel, or whatever it was. The Water-Eye. That's it! The Water-Eye! I remember now. Shaklat had four Eyes: Earth-Eye, Air-Eye, Fire-Eye and Water-Eye. (How stupid.) And he had a tongue of flame, and he was a Servant of the Sun, and when the Armies of Darkness rose up against him he defeated them by bringing the sun down to earth, and scorching the land until it was a desert. And when the great fire had burned out, all that was left of Shaklat was his Water-Eye, which was hidden away in a desert temple.

The Water-Eye. I wonder if it's some kind of jewel? They say it's going to restore the desert to pastureland, when it's found again, but that sounds like a lot of old dung-cakes to me. It sounds like the sort of thing you'd tell your grandchildren at bedtime, to make them feel better about the heat and the dust and the sandfleas and the fact that there's never enough to drink.

Mmmm. I could do with a drink.

One careful step forward, and another, and another. The stones crunch under my feet. They roll down the side of the pit, reaching the bottom before I do; they seem to make a terrible noise in the silence. Still nothing stirs. You don't think it's a trap, do you? A sand-trap? But this isn't sand-trap terrain – too many rocks and footholds. The first piece of shell is shaped like a hook, and there's a layer of dust over it – several months' worth of dust. Yeowch! It's burning hot! It's ... it's *metal*. It's made of metal, like a saucepan.

Surely that whole thing can't be made of metal?

I don't believe it. This is too strange. Lizards don't lay metal eggs, and men don't build metal houses. Who could afford a metal house, except someone who was swimming in gold? Someone like ...

Someone like Shaklat.

3

Perhaps I should go. If this is magic, I'd better not interfere. But surely the Temple of Shaklat would be buried in dust? Surely you'd have to dig for it, the way I dug for those amulets this morning? The Temple of Shaklat would be as old as my amulets – older – and the desert always hides its secrets. On the other hand, if this really *is* a magic temple . . .

Oh curse it, Jansi, make up your mind!

The door is there, right ahead, with nothing but darkness beyond. If I were to light my torch, and take a peek – not a step, just a peek – then I could see what lies in the shadows without endangering myself. Because there might be a treasure, and I can't walk away from a treasure. It's been three days since I found any dragons' eggs; if I don't bring something back soon, the Caravan Master will stop feeding me. I have to pay my way. A scavenger's no use unless he can scavenge.

Let's see, now. Here's my tinder-box, and here's my lamp. I'll just rub and rub and rub and *there*! A flame. The lamp ignites. The heat is unbearable. I'll have one quick look . . . just to make sure . . .

2

471\3AA4\7\62:891

A boy is coming.

His height and bone mass, the elasticity of his skin, the minimal growth of hair on his jaw and upper lip, suggest that he has barely reached puberty – if the people of this planet follow the same growth cycle as that of the Rodanese. Evidently their culture is more primitive than Rodan's, for his clothes are not efficiently designed. The fastenings are inadequate; there is no heat-sealing or polarisation. The clothes themselves seem to be made of epidermal matter (some form of animal skin?), as well as fleece or hair modified to resemble plant fibres. They impede his movements; there are too many layers, poorly insulated. But perhaps the clothes of these people fulfil other purposes, besides protection. Hedda has told me about the decorative impulse. I would, for instance, speculate that the beads in his hair are ornamental, rather than practical, or that they classify him in some way. As for the length of his hair, it is most impractical. Hair of that length would be hard to keep clean.

He is moving very slowly, keeping close to the ground, looking in this direction. He appears to be carrying no supplies – no food or water. This would suggest two possibilities: either he has left his food somewhere out of scanning range, or he has come from a small community that is also out of scanning range. The community is probably mobile, because if it were fixed, one of its members would almost certainly have appeared before now. It has been two hundred and seventy galactic days since my arrival, and this boy is the first cognisant life-form to have manifested itself. I need this boy. I need his hands.

He is coming closer, but at a very slow speed, stopping every so often to squat down behind a rock or hummock. The slow speed could indicate several things: illness or injury; reluctance; caution. It is possible that he is using the rocks for concealment, in which case his slowness stems from alarm or fear. This would conform to the 'primitive behaviour' specs in my database. Primitive cultures usually fear anything new: Hedda told me that several times. She stressed the need for care when dealing with them. So I must be careful.

The boy is watching, his attention riveted to the Bio-cell. He has brown eyes, like Deel's, but this is of no significance. His skin is darker than Deel's. Dark skin can mean intensive exposure to the sun, but not in every case. The boy's teeth are in poor condition. He is missing the tip of his right index finger. There is an infected pustule on his cheek, near the bridge of the nose.

He is still watching.

If Deel were here, he would suggest ways of luring this boy into the Bio-cell. Possibly a sweet smell – a smell of food, for instance – might encourage him to enter. Some kind of sound might also attract him: music, perhaps, or a cry for help. But a cry for help would be difficult to engineer, without knowing his language. It might also scare him away. I cannot risk scaring him away. I will do as Hedda would do: I will wait and watch. I will collect my data before I act.

He is moving forward, placing his feet carefully, heading for the airlock. He stops. He opens a small receptacle hanging from the strap around his waist, and removes two implements. The friction he produces by rubbing one of these against the other is enough to create a short-lived flame, which he applies to the lamp that also hangs from his waist. (A primitive lamp; the technological development here must be very modest.) Thrusting his lamp into the airlock, he peers around the edge of the door as if to ascertain what lies within. Should I activate the lighting system? No, not yet. Not until he comes inside. Inaction has so far proved the most successful strategy, so I shall remain dormant. I shall 'keep my head down', as Deel used to say.

The boy is exhibiting signs of disturbance. His hands are trembling. I would deduce that his lamp has a very limited area of irradiation – that he can see very little from outside the airlock. This could work to my advantage. He will be forced to come inside, if he wants to see anything. He has already placed one foot on the threshold.

And here comes the other foot. He is standing inside the airlock now, but I shall wait a little longer. The door of the airlock takes 3.47 seconds to close, and I have no information on the speed that this boy might attain when he is propelled by adrenalin. For he will almost certainly try to escape if I try to restrain him; that much I understand from my generic behavioural profiles.

The boy takes a few more steps, squinting into the darkness. He is carrying a knife in one hand, its blade uplifted. I wonder what the purpose of that is? Protection? Food preparation?

Time to close the door, I think.

'Aieee!' He swings around, but my calculations were correct; he cannot reach the door before it shuts. Ignorant of its strength, he flings himself against it, pounding and kicking in a way that might hurt or disable him.

'The door will not yield, boy. You are running a needless risk.'

He screams, and continues to strike the panels; clearly my words have had no effect. The most likely reason for this is that he does not comprehend Galactic Standard Speech. But my databanks contain a complete mastery of two hundred and eighty-seven languages, together with nine hundred and sixty dialectical variations. It is possible that he will understand one of these. The Gethr tongue, for instance:

'Rayak nipal, la. Bieyn seriyallet synak ocho.'

No success there. In fact it seems to be having the opposite effect. Perhaps I should activate the lighting system; he has dropped his lamp, and people often behave abnormally when deprived of the full spectrum of light. (Hedda preferred to have a light on even when she was asleep.) The boy is speaking now, sitting with his back against the bulkhead, breathing heavily. He seems to be repeating the same words, over and over again, but I cannot find a match for these words in my databanks. A most unfortunate state of affairs. It will be difficult if we have no mutual linguistic base. How will he follow my instructions if he cannot understand them?

And now he appears to be attacking the door with his knife. What futile behaviour; surely he can see that a knife will have no effect on reinforced iridium? Perhaps his reasoning skills are under-developed – he is, after all, from a primitive culture. Alternatively, his reasoning skills might have been affected by his emotional outburst. Perhaps he will be more rational when he calms down. Hedda always told Deel to calm down. *Calm down, Deel*, she would say. *You're not thinking*. And Deel would always respond well to that.

Perhaps if Hedda spoke to this boy, she might have a tranquillising effect on him. I shall play him my first interview with Hedda, and see what happens.

It is to be hoped that he will react more positively to a human face.

3

Someone's talking. Someone – but it isn't Shaklat. It's a woman's voice. I can't understand, I can't see . . . where is she? Help! *Help!* It's coming from over there! No, from over there. It's coming from the *ceiling*! Oh spirit of Emen, save your son. Please, Emen, please, I'm begging you. The voice drones on . . . and there's a face! It's her face, the woman's face, looking through a window. She's talking. She's smiling. She has golden hair, cut short, like a little child's. What does she want from me?

'What do you want from me?'

I can't understand her. She just talks and talks without making sense – staring out from that window, grinning, taunting, like a witch. A crone. 'Let me out, you witch! Let me out of here!' But she's still smiling, the sorceress. The snake. I'll show her. I'll get her. 'I'll cut you to pieces, you bitch! You'll die! You'll – '

Ah.

By the spirit of Emen. By the spirit of Emen, she isn't even there. She's a ghost. A shade. My knife . . . it passed right through her . . .

9

She's gone. Vanished. There's nothing left but a hollow in the wall. 'Let me go. Please. *Please.*' I've got to get out. This room – it isn't the only room. I can see more doors, three more, but they're all shut. The walls are white and shiny, like teeth; there are pipes on the ceiling. No windows. No hearth. The floor is as smooth as an eggshell. 'Lord Shaklat? Keeper of the Fire?' This door won't open. There's music in the air, strange music, music without players. Spirit music? The ghosts are all around, they've – yes! They've opened the second door!

But it's not a way out. It's another room, a smaller room, with a bed in it. Shaklat's bed? I've never seen anything like this. It must be the Temple; what else could it be? The floor is scattered with strange objects: a pear-shaped thing, a boot-shaped thing, a thing that could be a comb. It *is* a comb, I know it is. (The woman's comb?) And beyond the bed lies an even smaller room, a room full of white things like huge pots growing out of the floor. Aiee! And a mirror! A mirror as big as a rug! I've never seen a mirror so clear. It must be a magic mirror.

'Lord Shaklat?'

No reply.

'Lord Shaklat – please – if it is you, I meant no harm. I'm no one. Nothing. I'm a scavenger, Lord, I was passing by.'

The voice has stopped. The music has stopped. Is he listening?

'Please let me go, Lord, I'm not a hero. I'm not even a mage. You don't want me here, my blood is tainted. My mother was my father's sister. When I was born, they left me to die on the steps of the Round Hall at Sheboor.' Do you understand what I'm saying? I'm no threat. I'm not even a Citizen. 'Lord, I'm only alive because I was strong. I cried for two days, and my – my Choice-Father, Emen, he was lying sick nearby. He was feeling weak, and he had no sons to look after him. He thought: when I'm old, I will need a son. And he could hear that I was strong, so he took me from the steps.' Are you here, Emen? Is it your spirit, tormenting me? Will you plague me in death the way you did in life? 'Lord, you must let me go. If I don't get back, the caravan will leave. I have to join the caravan before sundown!'

Wait. What's that smell? It smells like food. Is someone cooking? Back in the big room, the smell is even stronger – sharper – and I can see where it's coming from. There's food on a shelf: red beans in gravy. Are they real beans, or ghost beans? They smell real. They look real. They're steaming and bubbling, as if they've just left the hob.

But I'm not going to eat them. You'd have to be a fool to eat enchanted beans.

'Lord? I'm not hungry! I don't want your food, I want to get out!'

The woman is back. She's sitting in her hollow. She looks very small – how did she become so small? She's eating, too, but I can't see . . .

Oh!

She's turned around. So quickly! How did she do that? And now she's bigger, and her spoon is bigger, and I can see what she's eating. Some kind of rice, with nuts in it. She dabs at her mouth, and smiles, and drinks.

Why is she doing this? What does it mean?

'Have mercy, Lord! You don't want me, I have no clan! I have no name! I'll pollute your Temple!' I've got to get out of here. I've got to *force* my way out. 'Let me go! Let me go, let me go, let me go – '

Whomp! The door won't yield, not even to this thing – this box, this seat, whatever it is. *Whomp!* Not a mark, not a dent, and the box is cracking. *Whomp!*

'Aaagh!'

A torrent of water, pouring onto my head.

4

6389\76-1104:56\44\3

This boy will injure himself.

Nothing seems to calm him. The music was ineffective, although it was Hedda's favourite song; she listened to it whenever she wanted to relax. Her image only makes him more agitated. He did not respond well to the food, even when I showed him how to eat it. Perhaps it does not appeal to his taste. Perhaps he is not hungry. There are so many variables in human behaviour – I find it difficult to interpret.

Whomp! And now he is striking the airlock door with a piece of duct casing. *Whomp!* This cannot continue; the duct casing was not built to withstand such force. Its structure is already breaking up, and when it disintegrates, the dispersion of fragments could be quite explosive. The boy may be hurt. I must prevent this.

But how? I cannot speak his language. I have no way of restraining him. To gas him would be inappropriate; Hedda always said that gas must be used only in the absence of any possible alternative. She called it a 'last resort'. She would not approve of gas.

I must think like Deel. Deel had many ideas. He would know how to quell an emotional outburst like this, because he used to succumb to such outbursts himself. And when he did, he would spend some time exercising. Or breathing deeply. Or having a bath . . .

A bath. Of course. I shall activate the extinguishers.

'Aaagh!'

The boy drops the duct casing. He runs from the cascade of water, but there are twenty-seven extinguisher nozzles in this room; he cannot escape them all. Squatting down behind the table, he covers his head with his hands. It appears that his emotions have subsided. I shall deactivate the extinguishers now.

I shall activate the drying currents instead.

'Naa!' The boy leaps up. Another emotional outburst? He springs away from a stream of hot air, and runs into Deel's room. It is difficult to understand why. Surely he cannot prefer to remain damp? Or does he dislike the sensation of hot air? He curls up on the bed, his face hidden.

I am picking up sensor readings from that bed: an accelerated heartbeat, and general muscular spasms. These might be manifestations of fear, although they can also result from exertion or sexual excitement. His physical attitude – curled up like an embryo – would perhaps suggest that fear is the cause. For this reason, I shall refrain from activating the drying currents in Deel's room; obviously the boy finds them disturbing.

I must find a way of reassuring him.

Some of Hedda's 'tranquillity tapes' might help. I shall play the *Lakes and Lilies* compilation. Hedda always said that pictures of water and waterfowl were refreshing to the spirit. Naturally, such pictures will have no effect unless the boy uncovers his face and looks at the viewer – but doubtless he will, in time. Meanwhile I must construct a hypothimage. Since it is evident that this boy's language is unlike any other in my

13

databanks (not surprising, when you consider how isolated his planet is), I must try to communicate with him in pictures, rather than words. I believe I have all the necessary recordings to construct a hypothetical image. I have viewed this boy now from every angle, and have made complete measurements of his hands and face; I can extrapolate from these, working from the data patterns I already possess, to create an image that will help to explain what I require.

If I construct an image of the boy, showing him in the act of fixing my relay/reception unit – splicing the damaged circuitry, and so forth – then perhaps he will understand that this is what I want him to do.

Of course, it will take some time; I am not well practised in the techniques of hypothimaging. It is a specialised field, which demands a very detailed knowledge of the way the human brain processes visual information. But I am confident that –

What is the boy doing now?

He has risen, and is dragging the sheet from Deel's bed. He takes it into the common room, where he pushes it against the base of the airlock door. His activities admit of no explanation. Does he intend to sleep there? Now he is applying friction to his fire-lighting equipment, which produces a small, sickly flame. Crouching down, he holds this flame to the sheet in a manner which suggests that he wants to ignite it. I find such behaviour completely illogical. A fire in the common room would only hurt him – and in any case, regulations prohibit the use of flammable fabric in the manufacture of bed-linen. Surely similar laws must apply on this planet?

If not, the number of fatalities must be considerable.

As was to be expected, the boy fails to light a fire. His first flame is extinguished; so is the second, and the third. He makes short, explosive noises that are very similar to the noises Deel used to make when he was disappointed with an analysis result.

Suddenly the boy throws down his fire-lighting equipment, and kicks the door, and shouts. There is moisture in his eyes. He extracts a small rock from somewhere beneath his layers of clothing, and hurls it at the Gravity Stabiliser.

Fortunately, the damage is minimal. But he has another rock now; this one bounces off the food dispensary. (If it had been aimed a little higher, it would have cracked the selection pad.) I cannot allow this. The Bio-cell's state of disrepair is bad enough without this.

I must activate the extinguishers again.

5

'All right, all right! I'm stopping! I've stopped!'

Water! Ugh! Water everywhere: in my ears, my nose, my mouth; pouring down my back (I can feel it) and into my boots. So much water ... where does it come from? How can it rain like this, inside a building? I *must* be in the presence of the Water-Eye.

'Don't do this! I'm sorry! I won't throw anything else!'

Little holes open up in the floor to let the water out. Hot air, like a desert wind, scorches my ankles. The rain has stopped. Where do those holes lead? But they shut like mouths before I have a chance to look.

There's a picture on the wall again; not of the golden-haired woman this time, but of a lake or river sparkling in the sun. It's like the view from a window, except that it keeps changing – from a lake to a bird to a floating flower, and back to the lake. What does it mean? I know it isn't real; it's like a dream or a vision. Am I dreaming now? Will I wake soon, and find myself rocking along with the caravan? Sitting at the tail-end of that long, scattered line of swaying animals, some laden with men, some with grain, some with water, as the Caravan Master sets the pace with his high, insistent chant?

But this isn't a dream. It's too wet to be a dream. I'm really here, in the Temple of Shaklat, and that hollow – that window, that thing on the wall – with its lakes and flowers and birds . . .

Could that be the Water-Eye?

'I don't want your Eye, Lord!' (It's hard to speak over the roar of hot air.) 'I haven't come to steal anything, I just want to go!' You couldn't steal that Eye, in any case; how could you steal a hollow in the wall? It would be easier to steal a sunset. Or a sigh. Or somebody's grin. This Eye is no jewel – it's a rainbow. A sunbeam. 'I won't tell anyone! I promise I'll keep everything a secret!'

No response. If only I could remember the stories. I remember about the Eyes, and the Temple, and the Ember Lord . . . but what else did the legends say about this Water-Eye? What happens when you discover it? Are there tests you have to pass? Spells you have to break? Fire is no good against water; I've seen that already. Perhaps my amulets would do the trick. Perhaps there's a special reason why I found them this morning. Could my amulets be keys to the Temple door?

There are three of them: two whole and one broken. The biggest is round and red, with mysterious marks engraved on one side. When I hold it up, nothing happens. The second is long, and has a hole in the middle. Still nothing. The third is in three pieces, and –

Wait. Wait a moment. What's that?

That's *me*!

Up on the wall – right there, on the Eye. It's me. I'm up there, walking on dirt, shuffling, crouching, I'm out in the sun. How could this be? I don't understand. It's my cloak and my tunic, my hair, my boots . . . but I recognise this. This has already happened. This is when I came down into the pit, when I was approaching the Temple. See! Look there! I'm taking out my tinder-box! I'm lighting my lamp! I remember all that, I remember doing it. And that's me coming inside, and that's the door closing, and that's my scream – my scream! I can hear myself!

'Aiee!'

Is that my voice? It sounds so odd.

'No! No! Let me out!'

And there's the woman's voice, and there I am with my knife – I look very stupid, very wild and foolish – and why does the picture keep changing? Sometimes I'm shown from above, sometimes from the back, sometimes from below, as if the Eye has been moving about. But the Eye doesn't move – or are there many Eyes? And what do these pictures mean? They're pictures from the past, the past living again, like a memory: a memory shown on the Eye. Shaklat's memory? Could Shaklat be showing me his memories?

But why would he do that?

Now I can see me in the small room with the mirror. (So there *must* be another Eye!) My voice again, so high and sharp: '... *I'm no one. Nothing. I'm a scavenger, Lord* ...' How strange I look from that angle; how dirty and dark against all the white. How long my nose is. My mouth moves in such a stupid way, but I look strong. I look old. I could be fourteen or fifteen.

I still seem to be talking.

Ah! And there I am in the big room again. I'm smelling the food ... I'm picking up the box ... *Whomp! Whomp!* And there's all the water, streaming down – just look at my face! How funny it is! I'm running around like a rabbit, up there, diving into the other room, curling up in bed. It's just like watching someone else. And this is where I try to burn the sheet. And this is the water, again. And this is ...

What's this?

This is me standing. Me watching. When did this happen? I don't remember – oh!

I moved! I moved and it moved! If I put out my hand . . .
yes! Look! Now the Eye is a mirror! I turn my head down here,
and I turn my head up there. I stick out my tongue down here,
and I stick out my tongue up there. The Jansi up there is like
a shadow, copying the Jansi down here. How remarkable.

Could Shaklat be trying to tell me something? Perhaps he's
telling me that he sees all and knows all. But the Eye has
blinked; the picture has changed. It's me again, walking into
a room – I don't recognise that room. I'm pointing. Peeling
something off a wall. What's this? I don't recognise this. I've
never even *done* this! It's a lie, all of it! I don't – I can't – I'm
not going to look! You can't make me!

'No! No!' This is bad magic! I won't look, I refuse to look!
I won't look at something I haven't done yet!

6

579\66205548:3\22-1

This boy will not look at my hypothimage. He is lying on Deel's bed, his face buried in the pillow. Why is he doing this? Surely he must understand? I have played all my recordings of the past seventy minutes, to make it as clear as possible; I have shown him the past, the present, and the future – what he has done, what he is doing, and what he must do. How could it be any clearer, without words? Hedda and Deel would not have behaved like this. They would not have hidden their faces, or thrown rocks. Yet this boy is a human being, just as they were. Why is he so different?

Perhaps the answer lies in his social background. I must remember that he comes from what is, manifestly, a primitive culture. Perhaps the differences are not just technological, but behavioural as well. I shall check my databanks. I shall run a scan for the word 'primitive'. There will not be very much, of course; the explosion occurred some time before we were able to begin those exercises covering under-developed technologies and outer-worlds. But there could have been something that Hedda once said . . .

Why, Deel. You're looking very primitive this morning.

No. Not that.

I like it. I like those primitive, earthy colours . . .

No. Not that either.

Hedda?

Yes, PIM?

Why do you describe your need for hot milk as a 'primitive urge'? You are technologically advanced, well educated and possessed of a thoroughly balanced psychological profile.

Why thank you, PIM. As a matter of fact, I was joking. But there are certain basic drives or emotions shared by all human beings, wherever they might come from, and those are often called 'primitive' — perhaps because they're related more to animal instincts than to reason.

I see. And could you tell me what these basic drives are?

Oh . . . Fear. Anger. Sorrow. Happiness . . .

Fear and anger I understand; they are the human 'flight or fight' motivations. Sorrow is more difficult, but often stems from some kind of physical hardship (loss of family, loss of limb). Happiness is associated with laughter. I know that. Hedda told me that.

And now the boy is crying.

I can see it clearly; he is wiping away tears. He is making convulsive movements. I should be able to analyse this — it is a clue, of sorts. Tears are directly related to sorrow, although they are not often shed by adult human beings. I never saw Deel weep. Hedda only wept once — when she was dying. I believe her tears stemmed from the pain she suffered. (Deel would have suffered no pain; his injury was to the head, and his death was instantaneous. Hedda's internal bleeding lasted for some time.) It is more often immature humans who weep: namely infants and children. This boy is a child. It is logical that he should weep, if he is sad.

But why is he sad? He might be in pain; the sensors are picking up some bruising on his right hand, where he struck at the airlock door. He might be hungry (infants cry when they are hungry), or suffering some form of loss. Whatever the reason, I must try to distract him. A boy in tears is a boy unable to absorb and process instructions; I must divert his mind away from his sorrows.

What would a child of his sort find diverting? A song, perhaps? A game?

Children like to play games.

Hedda?

Yes, PIM.

Why do you call the Skimmer 'childish'?

Because it's a game, PIM. Children like to play games.

The Skimmer. Of course. I will show this boy the Skimmer. It still lies in Deel's clothes-cupboard, among the weights and gravity boots and musical instruments. If I bang the cupboard door sharply – thus – it might catch his attention. No? He does not lift his face, but simply wraps his arms around his head.

Two more bangs, however, and he looks up to see what is happening. He notices the cupboard, which is standing open. He watches it for 3:02.16 minutes. Finally he gets up, and moves over to it.

I must wait. I must wait until he touches the Skimmer. He seems more interested in the clothes, although his interest is hampered somewhat by an obvious reluctance to make contact with anything. He keeps reaching out, then pulling his hand back, as if concerned that the harmless objects in Deel's cupboard might be dangerous. At last he fingers a sleeve, and finding it pleasant to touch, goes on to examine other things: the illuminator, the fluri-horn, the colourful cap. He seems very interested in the cap. I believe it has something to do with Deel's old school, although I was never offered any specific information.

At last he picks up the Skimmer. Now I can show him my recording.

Check this out, Hedda! I'm down to half a minute . . .

The boy jumps. He swings around, and adopts a crouching, defensive attitude which suggests surprise; was he unaware of Deel's viewer? But he is watching it now – the flickering movements of his eyes match the movements of Deel's image as it darts and lunges, trying to capture the weaving, hovering ball. Deel was very good at Skimmer. I can understand why it would be difficult for a species with such slow reflexes. The object of the game is fairly simple: once the ball is in the air, the player must pull it back into the shaft with magnetic suction. Of course, the ball is designed to evade capture, moving randomly through space at high speed. Deel once said that the concept was based on old hunting scenarios.

That is why I am convinced that the boy will understand and appreciate it.

He looks at the Skimmer in his hand, and back to Deel's image. I believe he might have made the connection. I shall focus on Deel's fingers as he flicks the activator switch on the shaft. Will the boy's mind grasp what this means? It appears so; he pushes the red switch, and the ball leaps into the air above his head.

What will his next action be, I wonder.

7

Another Eye! I thought as much. But is it the Water-Eye? Does the Water-Eye move from room to room, or is this the Earth-Eye? Perhaps all four Eyes survived Shaklat's inferno. Perhaps this is the Air-Eye, and it was responsible for the hot breath that followed the rain.

If there *are* two Eyes, then they seem to be possessed by different spirits. The spirit of the Water-Eye is that golden-haired woman, while the Air-Eye is possessed by this man – this dark-haired man. Or could this be Shaklat? He doesn't look like Shaklat. He only has two eyes, and no tongue of flame. He looks like an ordinary man: a stocky, broad-shouldered man with curly hair and pale skin. He's standing in this very room, this small room, and he's carrying the thing I'm carrying. What is it, I wonder? It looks like a cup-and-ball, except that I can't get the ball out of the cup. But it must be important, because I have a feeling – oh!

Look at that!

The man up there is running; he's running after the ball. The ball's in the air! It's floating like a bird, and it flits away from him, again and again. It must be a magic ball. He seems to be chasing it (he's very fast) but he has no net or sling. Why doesn't he try to grab it with his hand? This cup won't catch it – not unless he turns it upside down. Go! Yes! *Yes!* He's got it!

How did he do that?

And now he's doing it again. He pushes the red spot on the side of his cup, and the ball springs into the air. I don't understand this. What does it all mean? It must mean something; Shaklat opened the cupboard door, and showed me those things. He must have wanted me to see them – to see the clothes and the boots and the cup-and-ball. But why? For what purpose? Am I supposed to be doing something?

Perhaps that picture up there is a memory, not a spirit. Perhaps the dark-haired man was here once, standing where I'm standing, wearing those clothes and sleeping in that bed. If so, then he's gone now; he either died or escaped. And if he *did* escape, surely I can too? By doing what he did, perhaps?

Wait! I've got it! He's using the cup-and-ball – the same one as I have – maybe that's the key! Maybe if I capture the magic ball then Shaklat will let me go! Could that be the answer? Could that be what he's been trying to tell me? 'Is it some kind of challenge, Lord? Some kind of test that I have to pass?' Shaklat says nothing, but I'm going to do it anyway; I'm going to touch this spot and – there! The ball! It's flying away!

By the Spirit of All Things, this is a great enchantment. Look at the way it moves, just like a bee. Just like a fish. Now what does he do, the dark-haired man? He simply holds the cup underneath it – or tries to – whoops! There it goes! Whoops! And it's off again! You have to be quick, but I can be quick. I learned to dodge Emen's blows when I was still a suckling. As for the other men in our caravan, they liked to hit me whenever things went wrong – because I've always been the lowest of the low, lower even than our beasts of burden.

So there was never anyone faster than me.

'Got you!'

No. Curses. I missed. It's hovering there, taunting me, spinning like a wheel. I must think like a mountain-cat. I must concentrate on the ball, and let my hands take care of themselves. This is like hunting; it's like catching mice in a grain shed. *Yes!*

No. Missed again.

I wonder how long I've been here? Surely it can't be sundown yet? But the caravan must be stirring itself – Bhanrit must be wondering where I am. They'll give me until the sun's glow fades, and then they'll leave. I know I'll get a beating (I always get a beating if I'm not back before the sun sinks below the horizon), but as long as they don't pack up and go ... as long as I don't miss them ...

What if they leave me here? What if they think I'm dead? Bhanrit would want to search for me, because he's my friend – my only friend – but they wouldn't listen to him. He's only a boy like me, even though he *is* the Caravan Master's son. No one would risk wasting a night's journey for my sake. When you don't even bother to bury your dead on the road, when you leave them out for the Black Dragons, then you certainly don't wait about for a scavenger boy who's only with you on sufferance.

Stop. Don't think about that. Think about the ball. The sooner you catch this ball, the sooner you'll get out. See what happens? Every time you move, it moves as well. Perhaps if you pretend to step back, but only on one foot, and then lunge forward –

YES! I did it! Oh spirit of Emen! Oh joy of joys! I caught the ball; I sucked it down! Did you see that? Did you see what I did? I passed the test!

And now let me look. Let me check the big room – is the door open?

The door isn't open.

Perhaps if I push it ... come on. *Come on.* 'I caught the ball! You should let me out!' Where are you, Shaklat? Didn't you see? I caught the ball! *I caught the ball!*

'Let me out, curse you! I did it! I've got to go!' (May your Eyes be blinded, you monster!) 'If I don't go now, they'll leave without me! Don't you understand? I'm nothing to them, they won't come and look, they're *afraid* to look, they're afraid of the desert! There's nothing out there, can't you see that? Nothing! If I don't leave now, I'll be stuck here forever!'

Say something! *Say something!* The Eye blinks; a picture appears.

It's the picture of the floating flower.

Oh no. This can't be. I'm doomed. I'm finished. I'll never get back, I'm trapped here – I'll die here – what am I going to do? Why is this happening? Emen, you scum, you bastard, where are you? Why don't you help me? You're a spirit now, it's your *job* to help the living! For once, just for once ...

But I'm all alone. There's no one – no living family, no dead family. I have no ancestors; their spirits turned away from me when I was born. Why was I born? Why did Emen save me – just to treat me like a dog until his tiny, shrivelled heart gave out and he died without leaving me anything but his clothes? Oh Shaklat, have pity. Have pity on my wretchedness.

There is no hope left for me.

8

911\34-31333\0-79.1

The boy is weeping again. He has thrown down the Skimmer, and slumped to the floor. Why is he reacting like this? Whenever Deel won a point, he would laugh and punch the air; he never wept or tried to damage the Skimmer unit. This boy's responses are inexplicable. Even Hedda would find them hard to comprehend.

He is making very loud noises, the kind of noises that Hedda made before she died. Yet the scanners have picked up no life-threatening injuries. Could this be an example of the mental pain that Deel often talked about? Evidently this boy has little control over his emotional impulses – far less control than Hedda or Deel displayed. It may be some time before he is rational enough to understand what I want him to do. I should perhaps prepare myself for several days of his company.

It will be a useful exercise, to accommodate a human being again. My capacities in this respect have been unexploited for some time.

I shall begin with another offer of food; doubtless he must be growing hungry. Then I will encourage him to clean himself (he is in a most unhygienic state) and go to bed. The sun is very low outside; soon it will be evening. I shall scent the air, and play some of Hedda's bedtime music. Perhaps he would enjoy a hot drink? Unfortunately, the massage unit was damaged by the explosion – but even if it had survived, I believe I would have had difficulty making him understand what it was for. He seems incapable of grasping even the simplest concepts.

He is displaying no interest in the braised liver. I shall withdraw it, and offer the 'samyut' (stew), instead. He is lying on the floor now, still weeping, his face hidden. The samyut has a very rich, spicy aroma (or so Hedda told me), but does not elicit any reaction from the boy; I wonder if he lacks a sense of smell? Perhaps the human beings on this planet have a sustenance cycle that differs from that of Rodan. Perhaps they only eat once every couple of days.

I am sure that Hedda would soon find the answers to these questions. It is to be regretted that she is not available. But of course, if she were, I would have no need of this boy. She could have repaired the relay/reception unit herself.

Clearly my offers of food are unwelcome. I shall desist, and concentrate on urging the boy to wash. My recordings of Deel in the shower might be effective – if the boy would only look at them. But he simply lies there, his face buried in his folded arms. The loud noises have subsided; occasionally his body is shaken by a convulsive movement, rather like a hiccough. I have no information on what this means.

Of course, in one sense the boy has already been washed – by the extinguishers. An alkaline agent will be needed to remove all the dirt, but some progress has been made. It is possible that I should let him sleep first. Should I perhaps give him a choice of rooms? He might prefer Hedda's room to Deel's – or even one of the others. I shall open the doors for him.

On closer inspection, it is obvious that the boy is harbouring small parasites in his hair. These must be expunged. I can do so if he gets into the shower; certain chemicals can be added to the water supply. But he must be made to keep still. He must be made to rub his head vigorously. How will I encourage him to do this?

He is lying very still now. His breathing is slow and regular. He appears to be calm ... in fact, he appears to be sleeping. Without monitoring his brain waves it is difficult to confirm this, but every other sign points to the same conclusion.

How could he have gone to sleep on the floor? I was under the impression that human beings need beds – or at least chairs – to sleep in. Hedda and Deel would only ever sleep on beds or chairs. But this boy is from a primitive culture. Perhaps there are no beds where he comes from.

I shall not wake him; I shall let him sleep. Outside, the sun is sinking. Night approaches. I shall increase the air temperature in the Bio-cell and wait until morning, when communication might be easier.

Hedda always used to say that things look better in the morning. Perhaps this boy operates under the same principle.

9

What's that smell? Are we moving on? Is it time to . . .

Oh.

I remember. Shaklat. The Water-Eye. It's coming back to me now.

I was hoping that I'd dreamed it all.

Nothing looks any different. I feel so stiff from sleeping on the ground. Such an ache in my back . . . and my stomach is empty. Is it morning? It must be. It feels as if I've been asleep for a long time.

I suppose I must have missed the caravan.

There's food on that shelf again – something hot and fragrant. I might as well eat it; there isn't much choice. If I don't die from eating enchanted food, I'll die of starvation. And what does it matter, anyway? I'm as good as dead. Maybe I *am* dead. Ouch! My back! Except that ghosts don't bruise their spines by sleeping on the ground. I feel like a cripple. I can hardly walk.

The food is some kind of white mushy stuff in a bowl, but it smells good. It doesn't burn my fingers. And it tastes *wonderful*. It tastes the way enchanted food should taste. I'm not sure what it is (it's a bit fruity, and a bit grainy, and a bit like eggwhite); I just hope it's nothing repulsive. I just hope it's not ground-up babies' bones, or worm-spit.

The Eye blinks; there's that woman again, eating her rice. She's waving her spoon about. Am I supposed to use the spoon? I'm no good with spoons – I'm better with hands. Mmmm. Oh, but this is delicious. Even if it kills me, it's still delicious. It's sweet and creamy, and it slides down like oil. Maybe I won't mind staying here after all, if the food is this good.

Ah. That's better. I feel better now.

What's this? A drink? A cold drink . . . eech! So sharp! Acid! I don't like it – the way it burns my tongue. I don't want any more of *that* stuff.

The shelf is moving. It's going back into the wall, taking the bowl and cup with it. How does that happen? The bowl disappears, the cup disappears, and here comes the shelf again. With another cup! A steaming cup of brown liquid, different from the sour, acidic drink. This stuff is sweet and rich, and I like it.

So Shaklat will give me what I like?

'Can I have a honey-cake, Lord? Honey-cake?'

No response. The Eye is making pictures again, but I don't want to look, not at those pictures. Those pictures are bad magic. I've never done any of that – it's a lie, a spell. It scares me.

I'm going to have a piss.

Where shall I do it? In a corner? Maybe in one of the other rooms. All the doors are open now, except the one that leads outside, and that one near the Water-Eye (I wonder what's behind it?). There seem to be so many rooms, all white and shiny, windowless, spotless. This one has a bed in it, and a rug in it, and a cushion. The cushion makes me feel better.

Someone *must* have been living here – someone who used the little glass bottles that are smashed all over the floor. The red and pink stains must have come from the stuff in those bottles: a powder, of some sort, and a dried-up liquid. There are stains on the wall, as well as on the floor. There's something small and blue under the bed.

It looks like an animal, a toy animal made of wool, with two ears and shiny black eyes; it feels soft when you squeeze it. The sewing is very clumsy. Who could have made this? The golden-haired woman? The dark-haired man? Or did it belong to someone else – a child, perhaps? It smells of perfume, and someone has drawn a mouth on it, in black, smiling. I wish I knew what kind of animal it was. I wish I knew who left it here.

My bladder is full.

If I ever get out, I think I'll take that toy with me. For now I'll just put it down here, on the bed, while I relieve myself. This room can be my cesspit. I'll keep the door closed, so it won't smell up the other rooms, and maybe if I –

WHAM!

What's that? What's that noise? Help! It's the cupboard door, banging and banging – and there's an Eye! *Another* Eye, showing another picture.

It's the dark-haired man again, opening his clothes. He's pissing! He's pissing into one of those giant white pots that I saw in the little room. Hah! Now I know he's not a spirit. Spirits don't piss. He must be a man too, and he must have lived here. Maybe he lived here with that golden-haired woman. Maybe they had a little child.

What's Shaklat trying to tell me with this picture? That I'm allowed to piss? That I must piss into the white pot? Maybe that's what I should do. It certainly makes sense. I'll go in there, through that door, because there's another little room behind that door, with another white pot. And look! There's even water at the bottom of the pot. Water, not piss. I wonder what it's there for?

Let's hope there isn't an Eye in this room. I don't want Shaklat to watch me piss, although he probably will; Shaklat sees everything. If he saw the dark-haired man doing this – if he remembered the dark-haired man emptying his bladder – then he must certainly have a good, clear view of me.

'Aiee!' What's that? The piss has been sucked away! The water's been sucked away!

I'm getting out of here.

10

700.12\64-45900101\6

I believe that I am making progress. The boy has eaten, he has drunk, and he has disposed of his waste in the correct manner, rather than (as I at one point anticipated) expelling his urine all over the floor of Hedda's room. He seems calmer than he did yesterday; he is exhibiting signs of interest in his surroundings.

Yet he still refuses to look at my hypothimage.

What is his objection? He appears quite comfortable with every other image I have played – my recordings of Hedda and Deel, for instance. He will even look at recordings of his own activities, as long as those activities are from the past or present, rather than the projected future. He is back in Deel's room now, fingering the tooth-spray. I shall demonstrate how it should be employed.

The fact that the head of the tooth-spray can only be activated when it is inside somebody's mouth does, of course, make a clear demonstration rather difficult. I doubt that this recording of Deel will leave the boy any wiser. Nevertheless he watches it for several minutes before returning the machine to its slot. He does not attempt to follow Deel's example.

Now he is picking up the depilatory stick, which is, of course, activated by touch. He drops it as it begins to whine; clearly the noise disturbs him. But the image of Deel shaving seems to interest him enormously, and he follows Deel's movements with careful attention, his brow puckered, before retrieving the stick and applying it gingerly to his face. Obviously he finds the sensation unacceptable – unpleasant, perhaps? – because he flinches, and eyes the stick with an expression that I find difficult to interpret (despite the fact that it is, like many of his expressions, more extreme and emphatic than Hedda's or Deel's ever were). After a few minutes he applies the stick to his arm, removing some of the fine, black hair.

He mutters to himself.

This interest in objects around the Bio-cell is an encouraging sign, I believe. It is the sort of behaviour that one would expect from a rational intelligence. I do not understand why the boy is carrying Hedda's soft sculpture around with him (it was a gift from her niece, Galanas), but doubtless there is an explanation. I would even speculate that he is beginning to understand my efforts at visual communication; when he picks up a facial swab he turns directly to the viewer, as if expecting my explanatory image.

I can see an interactive mode establishing itself here.

Suddenly he stops beneath the common-room viewer, and says something. He points at his mouth, at the viewer, at his mouth again. He rubs his abdomen, just below the ribcage. He licks his lips.

Could he be asking for food? It would seem so. I do not believe that another serving would be beneficial just yet (diet must always be closely monitored against inactivity levels, for health reasons), but I have no objection to providing him with another drink. Since he appeared to dislike the juice, I shall supply him with another cup of Jentla Sweet-Sip.

When I dispense the drink he takes it, looks up at the viewer, and smiles. The smile is an indication of improved spirits – contentment – even happiness. It is, I believe, another encouraging sign, and one that suggests I have interpreted his gestures correctly. The inference is clear: I am beginning to communicate with him; he is beginning to communicate with me. I shall now play the auxiliary hypothimage that I created last night while he was sleeping: namely, my projection of the boy leaving the Bio-cell. If I play that, and follow it with an image of him repairing my relay/reception unit, he may realise that there is a connection between the two. He may deduce that one (the repair) will inevitably lead to the other (his release).

But so as not to overburden his limited intellectual capacities, I shall play only the first step of the repair process: his entrance into the Operations room.

'Aiee!' He is staring at the first hypothimage. As I anticipated, the sight of his own release – of his first steps out of the airlock – has attracted his attention. Although he looks away, he quickly looks back again, and watches himself climbing out of the crater with an alertness that testifies to his interest. It is fortunate that this hypothimage has been so effective; I found it a very difficult pattern to calculate.

Now he is watching himself enter the Operations room. By alternating this image with my hypothimage of his release, I shall emphasise the link between the first and second actions. He is still gazing up at the viewer – at himself in the Operations room, at himself outside, in the Operations room, outside, in the Operations room, outside . . .

He glances towards the door of the Operations room.

Now I shall open it.

11

Shaklat is trying to tell me something. Unless I'm mistaken, he's trying to tell me that if I walk through that door, that closed door near the Water-Eye, I'll end up outside. I'll be free.

But is he telling the truth?

I don't know if I should trust him; he's lied before, with his pictures of me doing things that I've never done. On the other hand, this is the first time he's actually shown a picture of me leaving the Temple – so perhaps it's some kind of prophecy. Perhaps the Eye can show me prophecies, as well as memories. I don't see why not. If Shaklat can conjure up food, and water, and magic wands that take the hair off your arm, then a little prophecy should present no problems.

The closed door is open now. Beyond it lies not the desert, but another big room, full of glittering jewels (or are they stars?): red and blue and yellow stars scattered all over the walls and ceiling. The air that flows out of this room is as cold as death; the light in there is dim, and the colours sombre. I don't like the look of it. Why is it so different? Why is it so cold?

The chairs and walls are black, like charcoal, while the air smells strange. Tainted.

Dead.

There's another Eye in that room, surrounded by stars, sitting up near the ceiling. (That makes four Eyes altogether.) It has a picture of me on it, but I can't quite see what I'm doing up there, not from this distance. Cold air nips at my nose. If I put something in the doorway – that box, for example – then Shaklat won't be able to trap me; I'll be able to get out if he tries to shut the door. (There. That should stop him.) My breath turns to mist as soon as I cross the threshold. I can feel my skin tightening.

There's something wrong with this room. It looks as if it's been disembowelled; knots of stiff, wiry threads are spilling like dried-up intestines from jagged holes in the wall. Pieces of glass crunch under my feet. I can see blackened stains, like scorch-marks, all over the floor and the –

What's that?

A long, glistening shape. A body. Oh spirit of Emen – oh spirit of –

It's her. It's her hair. Short, golden hair under a film of ice ... or is it glass? She's been encased, frozen; preserved like a dehydrated sheep's carcass on the caravan route to Sheboor. The blood on her mouth is still red. Her limbs are stiff and crooked.

One of her fingers has snapped off.

I'm going to be sick. No – I'm going to get out. I have to get out. I'm not staying in here, this is a charnel cave. Help! It's the man! I almost fell over him. His head is all ... it's all ...

Ugh.

He's dead. They're both dead. And Shaklat – Shaklat must have killed them. What am I going to do? I can't think ... I'm so scared ... 'Don't kill me!' Only one way out of this room, and that's the way I came in. 'Don't kill me, Lord!' I'm out! I made it! And I'm not going back in there – that room is cursed, it's a tomb, a graveyard. The cold breath and the black walls ... 'Oh please, *please* let me go! I'll do anything! Anything! What do you want me to do?'

Bow to him, Jansi. Make your submission. Grovel and worship; get down on the floor. 'You are m-my Master, Shaklat. All praise to the Keeper of the Fire. All praise to the Servant of the Sun. My heart is yours, and my hands, and my tongue – I am dust beneath your feet, Lord – '

Voices! I know those voices. Up on the Water-Eye, that woman is living again; she's sitting in the death room, on a black chair, dressed in the same green garment that she still wears beneath her mantle of ice. Her fingers are moving among the red and yellow stars. She's smiling. Talking.

The dark-haired man passes before her. He's drinking from a cup, and showing his teeth in a grin. They seem so calm and happy in that terrible room. They seem to understand it. They have to speak firmly over a barrage of other sounds: squeaking sounds, clicking sounds, and a voice – the woman's voice. Only now the woman isn't moving her lips. She's talking, but she isn't moving her lips.

WHOMP!

What's that? What's happening up there? I can't see the woman any more, but I can hear her scream; everything seems to be lurching and rolling. There are flames. Sparks. There's water, and a high-pitched sound like an angry mule, and the woman's voice, still calm, so calm, even though the picture is going round and round.

The man seems to be falling, bumping against things, his face a mass of blood. He's dead already; you can tell by the way his head bobs loose. He keeps falling, tumbling, as the woman calls to him – or *is* that the woman? Yes, it's her. She's terribly afraid, sobbing and moaning, but she's also talking quietly, evenly ... it's as if she has two voices. Two voices, both speaking at once.

I don't understand this.

The woman is falling, twisting, bouncing off the wall, just like her friend. She's trying to protect herself, but she's badly hurt. And her real voice, the voice from her mouth, is the frightened one – the pleading one. Her other voice, the calm one, isn't coming from her mouth at all. It's coming from everywhere ... and from nowhere. It's a spirit voice. The voice of the Temple.

Shaklat's voice?

'What do you want, Lord?' This doesn't make sense. The picture keeps churning, rolling; the quiet voice keeps droning on; the people keep bouncing off walls, their limbs loose and floppy. 'What are you trying to tell me? I don't understand.' Is this a threat, or a piece of advice? Is this what you *want* to happen to me, or what you *don't* want to happen? 'Did you kill those people, Lord, or did somebody else? Did you want them to die? Were they people like me? Were they prisoners, or servants? Did they want to stay here, or did you make them stay here?

'Please, Lord, please, I don't *understand*!'

12

29675548\1-123\44-3

At this point, Deel had just returned from the forward hold. He had been placing thermographs in the bays of each hold, to give us independent readings of the temperature fluctuations during our test schedule. (Although the ship possesses its own, built-in thermographs, they were being tested along with the climatic controls – therefore separate measuring units were needed.)

When Deel returned to the Bio-cell, I began to run the test program. The temperature in each bay dropped until it was the normal temperature of space vacuum: a fraction of a degree above absolute zero. It was then raised once more to its standard level, which, according to my databanks, was a couple of degrees below that of the Bio-cell. Hedda was checking my confirmations on the thermographic readouts as I adjusted the atmosphere in each bay.

Number 1, normal.
Check.
Number 2, normal.
Check.

Number 3, normal.

And . . . check.

Each hold contained one hundred and twenty-five bays, but only the first twelve bays of the forward hold contained any cargo. According to my inventory, this cargo was made up of medical supplies and circuitry prototypes.

PIM?

PIM's busy, Deel. Check.

Number 8, normal.

Check.

All right, but he can't be too busy to answer a question. PIM, when was the last time you ran a vermin sweep on that forward hold?

Number 9, normal. I completed my last vermin sweep exactly ten days ago, Deel.

Well I could have sworn I saw a rat in there.

Check. A rat! And what sort of a rat would that be, a 'space-rat'?

Could be.

Number 10, normal.

Check. Well if it was, it's not any more. I'm sure rats abhor a vacuum as much as nature does.

Number 11, norm —

WHOMP!

The explosion blew the forward hold to pieces. Because of its position between the two holds, the Bio-cell was also damaged. I have a full record of the destruction of my Repair Module circuitry – an image of my aft propulsion boosters flying off into space. The other boosters were, of course, deactivated, giving me no means whatsoever of restoring my flight path or even my centre of gravity. I was unable to correct the roll I was forced into, and damage to my relay/reception unit prevented me from signalling for help.

It is evident that the centre of the explosion was in the twelfth bay of the forward hold. All my readings indicate that

43

it was caused not by a malfunction but by a deliberately planted, rather sophisticated device. I believe this device must have had some sort of chemical ignition, which was activated by the drop in temperature, and then triggered when the temperature rose again.

I have no information on who could have planted it.

Fortunately my power-grid, short-sweep external visuals and Bio-cell atmospheric functions were not harmed in the explosion, so I was able to preserve the two corpses by means of a chemical coating and temperature adjustment. Apart from my navigational plotting, it was the last action I took for the next twenty-four days. I could skip forward to a later date now, and show the boy my entry into his planet's atmosphere (an entry which I endeavoured to slow by expelling certain stocks of gas at high pressure), but he seems to be losing interest in my recordings. He is looking away, and wiping his eyes.

Has he been weeping again?

Obviously the corpses frightened him; I have never seen a more perfect demonstration of the 'flight' reaction. He ran straight out of the Operations room, and is now sitting under the common-room viewer. His strange dips and contortions, earlier on, made no sense to me; they looked almost like exercises, but their timing was strangely inopportune.

I believe that my attempts to quieten his fears – to explain the presence of the crew's remains by showing him my recordings of their last hour – have been unsuccessful. It does not appear that he fully understands what he is seeing. Perhaps I should simply concentrate on his own role, and play my new hypothimage. It has occurred to me that by employing an additional human being (or at least the image of one), with all the expressive power of human gestures and facial contortions, I can more easily convey what I want the boy to do.

If Hedda shows him the way, then perhaps he will respond.

13

What's happening up there on the Eye? Is it another prophecy? The golden-haired woman is walking across this very room, walking, walking – and she's walking up to me! To *me*! By the spirit of Emen, don't tell me ... surely she can't ... is Shaklat going to bring her to life again?

Oh no, please, not that. I can't bear it; not a living corpse. I've got to get out of here.

She takes my hand. She leads me into the death room, and points at the wall. It's that same wall, the one I peeled open in the last prophecy. And there I am – I'm doing it again! I'm peeling it open, and looking at all the exposed intestines, and now she pulls a box out of the wall, a hollow box, and takes something from it. Oh! And here's a picture of her hand, holding the thing that she's just picked up – a very small thing, like a bone, only it's silver. She puts it in my hand, and points at the intestines.

Am I supposed to *do* something with those intestines?

Obviously I am. There's a flat, grey plate hanging off one of them – a tiny object, no bigger than my palm. The woman places it in my left hand, and guides my right hand towards it. Now there's a close view of the plate, which has raised lines drawn all over it in different colours; crisscrossed lines like the strings in a fishing net. The tip of the silvery, bone-like thing in my right hand seems to be counting those lines, from the rim of the plate down towards its centre. One, two, three, four, five . . .

On number six it stops. It runs along the line until it reaches a tiny, tiny break – a crack – and stops again, right over the crack, so that the crack is completely covered. The woman's thumb (so big in the picture) comes down and presses a round, black spot on the silver bone, whereupon the bone begins to vibrate. I wonder what this is all about? Is the bone really a key? Is the plate a lock? Is this a challenge of some sort?

Suddenly a red light flashes. The bone is pulled away, and the crack is gone. The line is whole again. It's been fixed, somehow – just like a real fishing net. Is this what Shaklat wants me to do? To fix this tiny fishing net?

Whoops! And here's another picture, a picture of me and the woman. The woman is smiling. She's patting my shoulder, and pointing at the door. She takes my hand and leads me out of the death room, out of the big room, out of the Temple and into the sunlight . . .

As I climb up the side of the pit, she turns and disappears back into the Temple. She doesn't even wait until I'm gone.

But I think I understand now. I think I know what Shaklat's been trying to tell me. He wants me to go back into that death room, open the wall, fix the little net on the grey plate, and leave. It's some kind of duty, some kind of rite which his priest and priestess can no longer perform, because they're dead. This prophecy is like a vision; a desire. A command. Once I've followed the command, I'll be free to go.

At least, I *hope* that's what he means.

'I'll do it, Lord. I'll do what you say.' And I'll do it now, before I have time to think – before I lose my courage. The death room is still as cold as frost; Shaklat is repeating his instructions on the Eye opposite the door. (He shows the box, the plate, the bone, the net.) And there's the real box! It's been pushed out of the wall – or dragged out, by invisible spirit hands – and it's sitting there, waiting for me. But I have to open the wall first. Now let me think . . .

There was a buckle in the picture, a buckle that I pulled . . . there! There it is! A golden buckle, fastened to the black wall. All I have to do is hook my finger through it, and pull down. Yes! A great slab of wall rolls away as easily as a length of fabric.

And there are the intestines, glistening like real guts. And there's the little grey plate. How small it is! The raised lines on its surface are as small as the lines on my finger. It's just as well I have good eyes; someone like Emen wouldn't have been able to see the *plate*, let alone what's on it.

Back to the box. It's still sitting there, black on the outside, white on the inside; it contains any number of little silver bones, all laid out in rows like plants in a vegetable garden. Which one should I take? Up on the Eye, a hand is choosing the second one from the left, in the top row, so I daresay that's the one I should be using.

But I have to pull hard to pick it up. You'd think it was stuck with glue, except that there is no glue. Another bit of Shaklat's magic.

Now – where's the sixth line? One, two, three, four, five, six. Here. The crack will be hard to spot, but if I hold the plate like this, so that the light casts a shadow . . . there. There it is. The smallest thing you've ever seen. Smaller than a grain of sand. Smaller than a head-louse. All I have to do is put the tip of my bone on top of it, and press the black spot – oooh! I can feel the bone shaking! It's like the feeling you get through your feet when a herd of animals thunders past.

The red light blinks; time to stop. And I can't see a crack any more, no matter how hard I look. The net is mended. The job is done. I'll put the bone back, and that's it – I'm finished. So what happens now?

There's nothing on the Eye any more. It's just a blank hollow, as dead as the woman on the floor underneath it. Out in the big room the Water-Eye is also blank. The light is dimming. The air feels dry. And the main door . . .

The main door is open.

14

01903\639-4127\0-1

The boy is gone. My relay/reception circuitry is repaired. I can now send out an all-frequency, long-range distress signal, with my position encoded in it. I cannot be absolutely exact about my position, because without any long-range relay/reception input – with only my short-sweep external visuals still operating – I had to rely on navigational plotting to calculate the course I followed after the explosion. But I am certain that this planet is the third in the system known as Rin32. And I would speculate that I am at a latitude of approximately 28 degrees, although such information will be irrelevant to any ship using my signal as a homing beacon.

I cannot expect a ship very soon, of course. This particular corner of the galaxy is almost unfrequented; it was chosen for that specific reason. All prototype models are tested in this area, to minimise any chance of unforeseen factors interfering with test schedules. For my own maiden voyage, it was particularly important that nothing unexpected should influence my Imprint. As a result, it may be some time before my signal reaches any ship or planet.

I would, however, anticipate a response within the next four hundred days.

Until then, I shall fight the corrosive effects of this weather system (wind-blown sand has already scoured the exterior of the Bio-cell), and review my databanks for any further information that might help me to understand the incident that threw me off course. There appears to be no logical explanation as to why someone should have planted an explosive device in the forward hold; the fact that it was there, however, suggests that the culprit was employed by Stelcorp – or Customs. It would have been impossible for an outsider to plant anything in my hold. The security for this particular test schedule was very tight indeed.

But who was the target of the attack? Was it the crew, or the ship, or both? Was it Stelcorp? I cannot understand why Stelcorp should come under attack: it is an efficient and safety-conscious organisation with the support of all five planets in the Galactic league. It maintains a satisfactory relationship with every domestic government body. There is every indication in my databanks that its control of the interplanetary travel and defence network is thoroughly endorsed by every authority that benefits from it.

Perhaps if I examine my recordings of the first thirty-six days of this voyage I shall find some remark, something said by Deel or Hedda, which will give me a clue. I must implement a search for discussions about animosity – because wholesale destruction of this type can only stem from a deeply felt hatred.

There are many words associated with such feelings: dislike, resentment, war, conflict, hostility, dispute, disagreement . . .

Deel and I have our own particular way of relating, PIM. We agree to disagree.

Yes, Hedda. You have pointed this out many times. But you have not explained what it means.

It means that although we might each have our own opinions on a

50

subject, we acknowledge that everyone has a right to their own views. Do you understand?

Not quite. Surely there is a correct and an incorrect view of everything?

Only of some things.

I find that difficult to comprehend.

Well ... let me try to explain. You know, don't you, that Deel and I tend to approach problems differently? We tend to think about them differently, and sometimes we come up with different solutions.

As far as I can ascertain, Hedda, the correct solution is always agreed on.

Sometimes, yes. But there may not be a correct solution.

That is illogical. A solution must always be correct.

PIM, I realise that it's very hard for you to think like a human being. You have your programs and your parameters. But what you have to understand is that when you look at Deel and me, you're looking at two people with different points of view. And sometimes neither of them is incorrect. They're just different.

If that is the case, then which one should I adopt?

At the moment, PIM, you should adopt the one I tell you to adopt. Later, perhaps ... well, we'll see. We have a lot of time to work it all out.

Nothing so far. But I shall continue my wordsearch while I plot the source of the vibration that has just entered my sensor range. It is light and irregular, but seems to be growing in strength; I am convinced that it is caused by the impact of approaching feet on dry earth. The feet themselves would certainly be within visual range if my position at the bottom of this crater did not impede my view of the surrounding countryside. If, however, my calculations are correct, the owner of the feet is heading in this direction, and should (if he or she does not alter his or her pace) appear at the top of the crater within the next 3:06.52 minutes.

I would speculate that the owner is human; certainly the

gait is that of a biped. It is possible that the boy has returned to his community and told his fellow inhabitants about my presence here. Perhaps someone is coming to check his report. It is to be hoped that the boy's people will react intelligently to my appearance, for primitive cultures will often try to destroy what they cannot comprehend. Of course, no primitive technology could possibly pierce the skin of my Bio-cell, but any attempts to do so would be undesirable. In fact any kind of mass contact at all would be undesirable; Stelcorp's policy is to avoid cultural interference wherever primitive technologies are concerned.

Perhaps I should have kept the boy here, rather than letting him go. But that would not have been humane behaviour, as specified in my databanks. Hedda, I know, would have disapproved. And in any case, it appears that the boy himself has returned: it is his face that peers over the edge of the crater – his shape that scrambles towards me.

He has been absent for exactly 204:59.22 minutes. Why has he decided to come back? It is unaccountable. A quick scan of the Bio-cell's interior shows that he has left nothing of his own behind, and I will not allow him to take anything of Stelcorp's with him. He falls over once, and moves as if something is slightly wrong with his motor skills: as if he has hurt himself, or is suffering from some form of shock. His colour is unhealthy.

'Shaklat,' he cries as he draws near. (That word again – he uses it quite often.) The rest of his speech is, of course, incomprehensible, but he is evidently disturbed, pounding on the airlock door and dropping to the ground as if his knees will no longer support him. Is this evidence of emotional or physical distress? What could have caused him to come back? There are several possible explanations: he might have lost his way; he might have been frightened or attacked by something; he might have been ordered to return.

Or could it be that he has nowhere else to go?

If, as I speculated, he belongs to a mobile community, it is possible that the community has become mobile again – that it has departed. In failing to anticipate this, I was seriously negligent. Depriving a boy of his cultural supports, of his friends and family, is an action verging on the criminal, according to my databanks. It would appear that I have not considered every risk. It would appear that I have demonstrated an unsatisfactory level of competence. Hedda, I believe, would be most disappointed.

All I can do now is to let the boy in, and make him comfortable.

15

'Jansi.'

Oh, go away.

'Jansi.'

Leave me alone! Can't you see I'm still sleeping? I need my sleep. And there's no reason to get up, anyway; there's nothing to get up *for*. No one's going to suffer if I don't get up. It's not as if we're in a caravan, or –

Oh. Curse it. He's heating the bed, again.

'All right, all right! I'm getting up!'

I don't know how he does it, but he does it; he makes the bed too hot to lie in. It's like trying to sleep on a skillet. The room is bright, and the music's playing – Shaklat's favourite music – and I need to piss. The question is, will I find the opening in time? I still don't understand these clothes.

'Aah.' That's better. The white bowl sucks it all down. Water begins to flow into the basin.

'Clean hands,' says Shaklat. Yes, yes, I know! You've told me often enough; I'm not stupid.

And now at last I can take off this awful outfit. I don't know

54

why he won't let me wear my own clothes to bed. I don't know why I have to wear *any* clothes to bed – it's warm enough not to. But Shaklat's will be done. At least he doesn't make me wear this thing all day, as well as all night. Perhaps he's being nice because my own clothes are so clean now; every morning, when I put them on, they smell of flowers.

Shaklat always has to clean everything. It's ridiculous how much he hates dirt.

'*Food, Jansi.*' Food, Jansi. My breakfast is waiting on the shelf in the big room. (It's that egg dish again.)

There are birds flitting around on the Water-Eye, but I don't want to see those pictures. I want to see the water pictures. 'Show me the boat. The boat.' He knows the word for 'boat'; his Eye blinks, and there it is – the boat on the water. All that water, all the way to the horizon. Nothing but water, and the fishing boat, and the fishermen hauling in their nets. I wonder where it is, that water? Could it actually be the sea? I've heard about the sea; I've heard that it goes on forever, and that if you sink into it you'll never reach the bottom. I've heard that it's like a lake, but not like a lake, because if you drink from it you'll die of thirst.

It sounds like magic to me. Perhaps that's why Shaklat has memories of it – or is this a prophecy, rather than a memory? Is this what's going to happen when the Water-Eye is un-leashed? Perhaps, instead of being turned into pastureland, the desert will be turned into water.

Mmmm. That was good. Delicious.

'Food, Shaklat. Food.' But of course he won't give me a second helping. He never does, unless I trick him. And he doesn't believe me any more when I pretend to faint; it took him a while, but he's seen through that little ruse. I'll have to think of something else.

Wonder what the weather's like today?

'*Teeth, Jansi.*'

'I just want to see what it's like outside – '

'Teeth, Jansi.'

Curse him; he won't even open the door. Why is he so stupid about my teeth? Clean, clean, clean – all I ever do is clean things. Back in the little room, my tooth-cleaner is chirping like a bird; it won't stop until I pick it up and put it in my mouth.

My own face glares at me from the mirror.

Perhaps it has something to do with the food in this place. Perhaps the food will poison you if it's not cleaned off your teeth. The Eye is showing pictures of me again, me and my teeth, as if I didn't know what to do already. I've only cleaned my teeth about a hundred and fifty times before, Shaklat!

'I've done it, all right? Can't you see I've done it? Look.' (Gnashing my fangs.) 'All finished.'

And now, if you please, I would like to go out. But the door is still closed. 'Out. Outside, Lord.' I'd better point, or he won't understand. He still hasn't mastered many words. 'Could you open the door, please?'

Ugh! What a wind! It charges through the widening crack like an invader; it rakes at my cheek with its burning claws; it howls and spits sand and tries to blind me. 'Close the door! Close the door!' Curse it, I can't go out in that. I'll have to stay inside today.

The noise fades as the door closes. The wind dies. The Eye blinks.

There's a picture on it.

'No.' Not that word stuff. 'Give me the hunting game. I want to play the hunting game.' But the Eye holds steady; Shaklat wants to learn more words. That picture – that mouth – can only mean one thing.

'Oh, all right.' (I don't really have much choice.) 'If you insist. But just a few, and then the hunting game. Ten words, and then the hunting game.' If I hold up both hands, he might understand. 'Ten words. Ten.'

The first picture is a picture of the sun, shining in a blue sky.

'Sun.'

He repeats the word: '*Sun*.'

The next picture is of a moon. A full moon.

'Moon.'

'*Moon*.'

And now here's the sun again, but this time it's rising – rising and setting. Rising and setting. Rising and setting.

What's he trying to say?

'That's a sunrise – and a sunset. Sunrise. Sunset. The sun rises . . . the sun sets.'

Silence.

'What? What is it? Isn't that what you want?' The sun rises again, quickly, and sets again. The moon rises, and disappears. The sun leaps into the sky. 'Oh. I see. Are you trying to ask me what the word for 'day' is? Is that what you want?'

'*Jansi sleep, Jansi awake. Jansi sleep, Jansi awake*.'

'Yes, yes, I get it. All right. Jansi sleep – night. Jansi awake – day. Day, night. Day, night.'

'*Day, night. Day, night*.' The sun rises. '*Day*.' The moon rises. '*Night*.'

'Yes.'

'*Day. Night*.' He's got it now. The Eye blinks, and shows a picture of me laughing. I'm laughing and laughing, over and over and over again. It's a memory of the only time I ever laughed in this Temple; the time when he showed me that picture of the little man falling down.

'Um . . . that's me. Jansi.'

Silence.

'I'm laughing. Ha-ha-ha. Jansi laugh. Jansi happy.'

'*Laugh. Happy*.'

'Yes.'

The picture changes. This time I'm crying. Yuk. I don't want to look at that. 'Jansi cry. Jansi unhappy.'

'*Cry. Unhappy.*'

'Tears.' If I point at my cheek, up there on the Eye, maybe he'll understand. 'Tears. Jansi cry tears.'

'*Jansi cry tears.*'

Oh my aching brain. This is so *boring*.

16

03\711549-6\26511-3

Jansi is becoming impatient. I can deduce this from the way he sighs, yawns, stretches his arms and wriggles about in his chair: all these actions are signals that he will very shortly get up and start moving around. He has an extremely short attention span sometimes.

Perhaps I should terminate the language program and play Deel's MasterShot game instead.

'Shaklat,' Jansi moans, kicking the bulkhead. Evidently he wants to tell me something: he always does when he uses that word. It appears to be his name for me, although what it actually means I cannot discover. He has been unable to grasp that my name is really PIM – or rather, that my nickname is PIM. I doubt that he even understands who I am. And it is difficult to explain, with no comparative terms of reference.

A grin creeps across his face as I download the first MasterShot Challenge.

'Lawan! Slegh, Shaklat!' he exclaims, and reaches for the controls. Considering his intellectual limitations, he has mastered the idea of the game very quickly. His reflexes are much faster than Deel's ever were, and his scores are much higher. But of course it is a simple idea, with clear graphics and a physical orientation. Naturally a person of his cultural background would respond well to the notion of fighting off and destroying a rapidly escalating number of armed enemies.

If I could persuade him to put on the Stimulator he would find it all far more exciting and realistic. But it is conceivable that he would not respond well to such neural rerouting. Events have shown me that it takes very little to disturb him, so I have tried to steer him away from anything with unstable molecular structures or sensory-distortion fields – anything that works by inducing hallucinations.

Time enough to show him such things when I have learned his language.

'Yaiee! Yai-yai-yai!' He is emitting more of those strange, high-pitched yelps, which I believe are associated with point-scores; he leaps from the chair and begins to strut about in the usual manner, jerking his head and throwing his arms about. I have come to the conclusion that these gestures are caused by the very emotions that moved Deel to punch at the air – they indicate that Jansi is very pleased with himself. Certainly his point-score is commendable. He turns to the controls with renewed vigour.

Outside, the wind has dropped. A shift in air pressure indicates that the atmosphere is becoming more settled.

When I open the door, however, he does not appear to notice.

'Jansi.'

He frowns.

'Jansi.'

'Naa!' he wails as I withdraw the MasterShot image. But he cannot be allowed to remain inside all day. Since he refuses to follow any exercise programs (largely, I believe, because I used Hedda to show him the positions, and he hates looking at

Hedda), he must exert himself outdoors. I do not want him to lose muscle tone. He is already responding well to an improved diet, and has grown perceptibly since coming here.

He is manifestly annoyed that I have terminated the MasterShot game.

'Siu maravel tynia, Shaklat,' he mumbles, folding his arms. The knitted brows, protruding lower lip and heavy breathing all indicate his state of mind; I have learned that the rearrangement of features on a human face – particularly Jansi's face – provides clear, visual information on the thoughts that are concealed behind that face.

But I shall feed him again before he goes, and that may improve his temper. He has an incomparable appetite. In fact he would eat all day, if I allowed him to – simply for the sake of eating.

'Aah!' he exclaims. As I suspected, he responds well to the food. It is one of his favourite dishes: rockfish salad. He pounces on it (using his fingers, of course – I have yet to persuade him to pick up a spoon), but almost immediately spits out his first mouthful.

'Yugh! Erk!' More spitting and grimacing. What can be wrong? Is the food unsatisfactory? He wipes his mouth and shakes his head; he puts the plate on his chair, and addresses himself to the viewer. (He always addresses the viewer. I suspect that he sees it as the source of all intelligence in this Bio-cell.) Clearly the food disagrees with him. Clearly something must have gone wrong, either in the cooking or the preservation process.

I shall dispense another plate of salad.

This time he swallows his first mouthful and goes on to finish the rest, licking the plate clean with his usual thoroughness. But after setting it down he turns back to the other plate, picks it up, and begins to eat. What is he doing? Surely that food is tainted?

'*Jansi. Jansi.*'

He looks up at the viewer, and grins. His teeth are covered in vegetable matter.

'*Jansi.*' I have no word for 'stop'. He is laughing now, and strutting about in that inexplicable, self-satisfied way that usually succeeds a perfect point-score. Once again, he is pleased with himself. But why? For what reason?

'Mmmm,' he says, sucking his fingers. It appears that the food no longer disagrees with him. Perhaps it never did. Perhaps this incident is related to certain previous ones (also associated with meal-times) when Jansi pretended to be suffering from low blood-sugar levels. Such a deception was, I believe, carefully designed to dupe me into dispensing more food – and I would speculate that I have just witnessed another successful attempt to do the same thing.

What a peculiar way to behave. One can only describe it as 'trickery'. I have never encountered trickery in any other human being, although Jansi seems to employ it quite often; this is the fifth time that I have detected him engaging in such behaviour. It is certainly effective. He wanted more food and he got it. I must analyse the various components of each incident, to understand how I might counteract any future attempts of the same sort.

And perhaps to establish whether I myself could make use of the odd 'trick' in my dealings with Jansi.

He is heading for the door now, still licking his fingers. Before reaching it he turns, looks at the viewer, and winks.

I have yet to ascertain the meaning of that particular facial contortion.

17

Of course there's no sign of a caravan. I'll keep looking (what else is there to do?), but I don't expect to find one. Caravans are so small, and the desert is so big. We were twenty days out of Ra-Holl, I remember, when Shaklat captured me, and how many times would a caravan visit Ra-Holl? Once a decade? It's such a dump of a town, Ra-Holl, with nothing to trade except bluestone, and precious little of that – so there's no reason for a trading caravan like ours to go anywhere near it. Besides which, bluestone isn't in great demand, and it takes a long time to shift bluestone. And a caravan depends on rapid turnover, because no one wants to drag heavy cargo back and forth across the desert.

No, I don't expect to see another caravan for a long, long time.

But I'm still going to keep looking. There's no harm in looking, and you never know – for once in my life, I might get lucky. Someone might cross my path. It would be nice if they did, because I'm sick of talking to myself. Shaklat's no fun to talk to, even though he has managed to pick up a few words: 'hand', 'mouth', 'foot', 'food', 'clean'. It doesn't make for very interesting conversation. Not that he hasn't been good to me – I'm not complaining. His food is wonderful, he keeps me warm at night, he shows me pictures and lets me play with his things. Only I get so lonely sometimes.

I wonder where Bhanrit is now? He's probably back in Sheboor, helping his father to trade that bluestone. Enjoying the markets, and the baths, and the singing of the women at sunset as they call their shepherd husbands back into the city before the gates close. I wonder if he misses me? I miss him. I wish I could tell him about Shaklat. I wish he had come with me, that last time – but of course his father wouldn't have let him. People with respectable parents don't go scavenging. Scavengers are low-caste, like the dogs that follow our caravan. Besides, parents are always afraid of Black Dragons and wind-devils, no matter how often you tell them that you've never seen a wind-devil in your life. And as for Black Dragons . . . well, people are always so stupid about Black Dragons. Most people never go into the desert – they always stay near the city, or the caravan – so they don't really know what Black Dragons are like. They hear silly stories, and believe them.

Speaking of Black Dragons, that's a very promising mound up ahead. Loose sand over dead grass. Sheltered. About the right size. I wonder . . .?

But there's no point, really. Shaklat can't cook lizard's eggs; I've already asked him once. And he won't let me build a fire in the Temple, so I can't cook them myself. It seems such a waste, just to leave them there. People in Sheboor would pay three or four chickens for one of those eggs – five for a big one. (Big eggs are in great demand for wedding feasts).

Hello. What's this? There seems to be some kind of movement beneath the sand. The grass fronds tremble . . . the sand shifts . . .

Glory! They're hatching! The eggs are hatching!

Oh, this is wonderful. This is so wonderful. I've never seen a hatching before. I wonder how long it takes? Surely not too long? But even if it takes until nightfall, I don't have to worry – not now. Not since Shaklat gave me his light-box. With a light-box like this you don't need anything else; you don't need to drop red stones to be sure that you'll find your way back again. All you have to do, if you get lost, is to wave Shaklat's light-box around, and when it's pointing in the right direction its little red eye will twinkle like a star. Shaklat is such a great magician. Imagine having your very own guiding star in the palm of your hand! And even if I lost it, I'd be able to find my way back, because he would light up the sky with his magic. He does that every time I stay out after dark; you can see it for miles. There are little suns all over his Temple, so bright that they hurt your eyes. They always guide me home again.

Hah! There it is! Another tremor. And a spurt of sand, as something digs its way out. Come on . . . come on . . . I've got to catch this one. If I do I can take it back to the Temple, and it will be my pet. A pet dragon! I bet no one else has a pet dragon. But I'll have to carry it there, somehow, and where shall I put it? In my cloak? They have sharp claws, these dragons – it might tear its way out. In my amulet bag? That's made of leather, so it should be strong enough. But will it be big enough?

Imagine returning to the caravan with my very own pet dragon. Bhanrit would be green with envy; they all would. And when it got big enough, no one would have the guts to beat me any more, because everyone would be much too frightened. In fact they'd be so frightened that they might not let me keep it. That's quite possible. There are lots of things they won't let me do. They won't let me eat or drink out of anyone else's vessels. They won't let me piss where everyone else does, in the camp. They won't let me talk to any girls, and they won't let me *near* the cargo, in case I steal it. The only thing they'll let me do is dig up eggs and amulets to trade – and even then they take half the profits.

When I leave here – if I leave here – I'm going to miss more than the food. At least in the Temple nobody beats me.

A twitch. A heave. A shiny head. *Got you!* Oh, it's so small – so small and so *strong*! A jewelled back. Gaping jaws. It's not going to fit in my amulet bag; I'm going to have to carry it home in my hands. Except that I'll never be able to climb that hill without the use of my hands.

Come on, Jansi. Think.

Here comes another one. It crawls out of the sand and disappears with a flick of its tail. I think I'll call this one Treasure. No – Jewel. 'Calm down, Jewel. No one's going to hurt you.' If I swaddle him like a baby so he can't move his limbs, and if I bind his mouth shut, then I'll be able to carry him under my arm. It's an undignified thing to do to a Black Dragon, but it won't be for long. And when we get back I'll build him his own little temple, and feed him from my own bowl (do lizards like fish?), and I'll have someone to play with. Someone to talk to.

Of course Shaklat will play with me, sometimes, but it's not the same thing. He's not really there. It's no fun playing with a spirit.

'*Ouch!* Jewel! That's *naughty*!'

18

111\39-31\7-8.2\5:391

I have never been able to understand why this boy collects so many functionless things on his excursions. The common room is now full of rocks, eggs, pieces of wood and ancient decorative items, none of which seem to interest him any more. But of all his discoveries, this one is without question the most incomprehensible.

Why bring back a living reptile?

It is quite obvious that the creature does not wish to be associated with Jansi. As soon as it was released from his garment, it shot across the room and concealed itself under a chair. When Jansi pursued it, the creature scampered along the wall and into a thermal vent. Of course, I could not allow it to stay there; a blast of hot air sent it flying into Jansi's arms, which I notice are badly scratched and bitten. Why attempt to restrain such a vicious animal? Why not let it go? It is clear that I shall have to alert Jansi to the purpose and whereabouts of the medical kit; if his wounds are not properly dressed, they will undoubtedly become septic.

'Jansi.'

He is crooning into the creature's ear. It is squirming and snapping; I can see the muscles standing out in his hands and wrists as he tries to hold it still.

'Jansi.'

He looks up. 'Lum,' he says. (That means 'food'.) 'Lum, Shaklat.'

'Jansi.' I will play the hypothimage I created, in anticipation of this moment: it shows him applying healant to a cut on his arm, and sealing the spot with a sterile patch. But he refuses to look – his attention is focused on the reptile.

'Jansi.'

'Lum! Yabbat lum!' he cries, pushing it towards the viewer. Could he be wishing to eat it? But he gets up, and stands beside the dispensary. 'Srit,' he says. (That means 'fish'.)

On reflection, I believe that a bite of fish will do the boy no harm. Perhaps it will improve his temper. But if he lets go of that reptile, I doubt that we shall see it again.

'Ouch!' As I anticipated, the reptile has taken advantage of his clumsy attempt to tuck it under his right arm. The pressure of its bite has caused Jansi to drop it; as he sucks his finger, moaning, it scuttles away into his room.

He snatches up a handful of fish, and runs after it.

'Jansi. Jansi.' If I cannot make him dress those wounds, it would at least be advisable to clean them. What he needs is a wash. But he ignores me; he is on his knees, peering into the narrow space between the bed and the floor, making clucking sounds with his tongue and waving the fish in front of him.

'Lillin,' he chirps. 'Lillin. Cuk, Lillin. Li-illin . . .'

'Jansi.'

'Shhh!' He turns to the viewer, frowning, and puts a finger over his lips. I have no understanding of this sign. It could mean anything. But at least he is looking at the viewer.

'Jansi.' He knows what this image means. It means that he should have a wash. Nevertheless, he disregards my advice, waving his hand in a fashion that I recognise as dismissive. He is looking under the bed again.

I shall have to cleanse those wounds myself. I shall have to activate the extinguishers.

'Naa!' His reaction to the water is unprecedented, extreme – explosive. He is screaming at the viewer, and waving his arms about. He is pointing at the bed. 'Naa! Nort! Naa, naa!' The reptile suddenly emerges from its hiding place, and runs across the room.

'*RS4T-PIM, are you receiving? This is RS8S-GIP-18.*'

A signal.

'*RS4T-PIM, we have received your distress signal. Your position is plotted. We are heading your way – estimated time of arrival, 03.06.43902.*'

'This is RS4T-PIM. Received and understood. Over.'

There is no response; I expected none. If their ETA is 03.06.43902, then I would calculate that my confirmation will not reach them for another three days, minimum. And they themselves will arrive six days after that. Nine days plus twenty-five days ... it will be a thirty-four-day lapse between my signal and the subsequent rescue. An unforeseen piece of luck. I was not anticipating any kind of reaction for at least another sixty days – possibly longer.

RS8S-GIP-18. That would be Rodan Ship Class 8 Security/ Galactic Interstellar Patrol Number 18. A security ship. According to my databanks, RS8S-GIP-18 is under the command of Worrell Pinza Hynde and Brate Bassery. I shall review their records at once.

'*RS4T-PIM, are you receiving? This is RS8S-GIP-18 ...*'

Here comes the message again. It will undoubtedly be repeated, every few minutes, until superseded by another. I shall keep my receptors open. There may be instructions they want me to follow.

'*... heading your way – estimated time of arrival, 03.06.43902.*'

Jansi has returned to the common room. He has emptied all the weights from Deel's weight-box, and is busy lining the box with Deel's thermal underwear.

How am I going to explain to him what has happened? Or, more importantly, what will happen?

19

'Jewel! Where are you? Look – I've got some lovely fish here. Lovely fish ... oh come on, you stupid lizard, where are you hiding?'

I can't believe this. He's got to be around somewhere. Maybe I should build a trap – bait it with food and leave it overnight.

'Jansi.'

I never realised how many holes and cracks and corners there were in this Temple. It's a lizard's dream. How am I ever going to find him if he doesn't want to be found? It's not fair; I've even made him his own temple to sleep in.

'Jansi.'

Maybe he doesn't like fish. Maybe I should try something else ...

Whoops! What's happening? The light's gone! It's as black as charcoal – I can't see –

'Shaklat! Don't do this!' What are you trying to accomplish? Are you trying to scare me? 'Bring back the light! Bring it back!'

The Water-Eye blinks; there's a picture on it, glowing in

the dimness. It's a picture of me. I'm smiling – beckoning. What am I up to?

'*Jansi*,' Shaklat drones. '*Jansi*.'

'What?'

'*People, Jansi*.'

'Pardon?'

'*People, Jansi*.' The picture changes. It's still a picture of me, but I'm sitting in a corner of the big room. I look up and smile as two people walk through the main door. '*People, Jansi*,' Shaklat says, and the picture repeats itself.

I wonder what it's supposed to mean? People? What people? Is this a memory, or a prophecy? I don't recognise the people up there; I've never seen them before. The woman doesn't have golden hair, and the man doesn't have dark curls. I can't see their hair at all under their headdresses. They walk through the door, over and over and over again. '*People, Jansi*.'

And now the Eye blinks. The people disappear, and there I am again, staring down from the Eye. I'm holding up eight fingers and a thumb. '*Nine day*,' says Shaklat. '*People. Nine day*.'

Nine days? What about them? But he's showing me that couple again; they're walking through the door. '*People, nine day. People, nine day*.' There must be a connection.

Nine days ago I was right here. I didn't see any people then. So he must be talking about nine days in the future. Or perhaps just a nine-day period? Perhaps those two strangers were living here for that long.

Perhaps they'll be arriving at the end of nine days.

'People?' If I point at the door, and make a beckoning gesture . . . 'People come? Through door?' (Walking my fingers like a pair of legs.) 'People come in nine days?'

'*People come in nine days. People come in nine days*.'

He keeps repeating himself; I think I may have got it. I think he's trying to tell me that we're expecting visitors.

But what visitors? From where? 'What people, Shaklat?

Desert people?' Perhaps it's a caravan! 'Desert people come in nine days?'

The Eye blinks. He's shut it – no, it's another picture. A picture of the night sky, with stars.

'*Star people*,' he says.

'Star people?'

'*Star people come in nine days.*'

I don't understand. Star people? What are star people? Are they spirits? I don't like the sound of them. Suddenly the sky disappears, replaced by a picture of me. I'm dancing. It's a memory, not a prophecy; I remember doing that, just a few days ago, when Shaklat was playing some of his spirit music. Very good music, it was. Very lively. It made you want to dance.

'*Happy, Jansi. Laugh, Jansi. Star people come in nine days.*'

Oh. So it's good news, is it? The light blazes up again; the music begins to play; I'm still dancing up there on the Eye, grinning like a fool, twirling and swaying and jumping. Happy, Jansi. Laugh, Jansi.

I wonder . . .

'Shaklat?'

The music stops.

'Could you open that door, please?' I'm pointing at the death room. He knows the word for 'door' – and sure enough, it slides open. Normally he keeps it shut. I don't know why; perhaps he knows I don't like that room. Or perhaps he doesn't like it himself.

But I have to go in. I have to ask.

The cold air reaches out and tweaks my nose; it grabs my wrists and makes my eyes water. Inside the room it's very dim, but everything becomes flooded with light as soon as I cross the threshold. Both corpses are lying where I left them, fingers splayed, mouths open, eyes empty, rigid beneath their skins of ice.

I'm almost afraid to point at them.

'Star people?' My mouth feels stiff. 'Star people, Shaklat?'

'*Star people*,' he replies. And this time he's using the woman's voice.

20

59477-13\3.0-3.1\57-9

As I expected, the boy has lost interest in his reptile. In fact he appears to have lost interest in everything except Hedda's corpse. He has been sitting beside it for 23:12.10 minutes now; it is difficult to understand why. I do not recall ever having seen him sit so still for so long, except when engrossed in a game of MasterShot.

His hunched posture and spasms of shuddering suggest that he must be cold.

'Jansi.'

He sniffs. I shall tell him that it is time for bed; perhaps that will elicit some kind of response. 'Rull' is his word for bed.

'Rull, Jansi. Rull.'

He sniffs again, but does not move. Although the temperature in this room is too low for human comfort, I cannot afford to raise it by even a fraction of a degree – to do so would subvert the preservation of both corpses. Jansi must be made to get out, before prolonged exposure to the cold begins to affect his health.

His sniffing indicates that his health may already be affected; according to my databanks, sniffing is a symptom of aggravated sinus membranes. Now he is wiping his eyes. That may also be a sign of ill-health, although I would speculate, after close examination of his features, that Jansi is sad rather than sick. I believe he is beginning to cry – or to 'woon', as he puts it.

'Jansi woon?'

He nods. That, I know, is an affirmative action. It means 'yes'. He points at Hedda, and at Deel; he says something about 'star people' ('yeu pess'), but adds another word, which I do not recognise.

'Gda,' he says. 'Gda.' He gets up, puts his hands to his throat, makes choking noises, and falls back onto the floor, where he lies for a moment with his tongue hanging out. 'Gda,' he repeats.

Could 'gda' be his word for 'dead'?

I shall find out. I shall play him an image of a dead bird. A dead lizard. A dead fish . . .

'Gda!' he cries, pointing at the fish. 'Srit gda!' He swings around and points at Hedda. 'Yeu pess gda!'

'Srit gda – yeu pess gda.'

'Yai. Yai, yai.' He nods his head, and adds something about the star people coming in nine days. 'Gda?' he inquires, pointing at the door. 'Yeu pess gda?'

Unless I am mistaken, he is asking whether the rescue team will be dead. What an unaccountable thing to say. Why should they be dead? He stands there hugging himself, shivering, his gaze on the viewer. He seems to be somewhat disturbed.

I shall play a hypothimage of him shaking his head; it is the only means I have of telling him 'no'. (He often uses head movements: up and down means 'yes', side to side means 'no'.) I must reassure him that none of the rescue team will be dead – on the contrary, they will all be very much alive.

I shall tell him to laugh. To be happy.

'Halala, Jansi. Corro, Jansi.'

'Shaklat?' His voice is very weak. He says something about 'nine days', pauses for an instant, and with his eyes fixed on the floor whispers, 'Jansi gda?'

Jansi dead? What does that mean? His tone is interrogative; he appears to be asking a question. Surely he cannot be wondering if he himself is dead? The evidence all points to the contrary, even for someone with such limited reasoning powers.

Or perhaps his mention of nine days is significant. Perhaps he is asking not whether he is dead, but whether he will be dead. In nine days. Such a reading would make more sense – although not very much sense. I still do not understand the way his mind works. He has some very illogical ideas.

Even the sight of my hypothimage shaking its head does not seem to reassure him.

'Jansi halala. Jansi Corro. Rull, Jansi.'

With a bowed head and slow, dragging footsteps, he moves off to his room, at last. He does not even stop at the dispensary, where a hot snack is waiting for him. Could this be a manifestation of some kind of illness? Loss of appetite often is. He undresses, puts his clothes in the laundry chute, and steps into the shower. Although I have been following the dietary guidelines very strictly, his height/body-fat ratio is still somewhat unbalanced and he is very thin. I doubt that the articulation of his bones should be quite so clear from a glance. I am also uncertain as to the best course I should follow in the treatment of his scars. He seems to have an abnormal number of scars (sixty-eight, at last count), and I do not know if there is something I should be doing about them. According to my databanks, scars can be removed – but I have yet to establish whether their removal is advisable or not. I do not even know if they give him pain, and of course I have no means of asking him.

It will be good when the rescue team comes. I shall ask for

a linguistic decoder program — a specialised program, not widely available, but one for which I have an obvious need. With a program like that, I shall be able to ask Jansi everything I want to know: why he weeps, why he winks, whether his scars hurt him ... and, of course, why he thinks that he may be going to die.

It will make communication a great deal easier.

21

There's hardly anything showing – just a tiny bit of wall poking above the sand. Anyone else would probably have walked right past it. But not me; I know what to look for. A bit of wall, a fragment of pottery, even a certain sort of mound – they're all signs of habitation, signs that something else might be hidden under the sand: beads, knives, amulets, whatever.

Sure enough, this wall is bigger than it looked at first. It seems to go down and down, and when I reach the bottom I might actually find something. Maybe I'll find one of those rings. The ring I found two years ago fetched an enormous price in Sheboor. And I found it buried near a wall just like this one, only there were other walls nearby. It must have been a huge settlement. A city, perhaps. Like Sheboor.

Whew! I get so hot doing this. If only I had a real shovel, instead of a tiny spade. If only Shaklat had a shovel. But there are all kinds of things that Shaklat doesn't have. He doesn't have shovels or needles or axes; he doesn't have knives or rope or paint. It makes me wonder, sometimes, if he really *is*

Shaklat – because surely Shaklat would use a knife? I've found a lot of old knives, over the years, in ruins just like this one. Knives and pins and axe-heads, as well as amulets. The ancient people of this desert all seemed to use knives. So why doesn't Shaklat?

But maybe you don't need them if you have magic like his. (There! What's that? Oh no – it's just a pebble.) Although his magic hasn't been so good lately, I must admit. He said that there would be people coming in nine days, and it's eleven days since then and still no one has shown. A false prophecy, if ever I heard one. Not that I particularly care; *I* don't want the star people to come. They sound like trouble to me. He keeps on saying that they're good, that I should be happy, but I know what they'll do – they'll try to throw me out. They'll say that I don't belong in the Temple, because I'm not a priest, or a mage, or whatever you're supposed to be. Because I haven't got that ghostly white skin, and I don't speak their language.

Well so what? It's not my fault that their stupid friends died. Shaklat needed someone to fix that little net, didn't he? I've got as much right to serve him as any star people. And they can't be all *that* keen to serve him or they wouldn't be so late arriving.

Gnnngh! That's a big rock. I'll just roll it over there. Now – where was I? Oh yes. Star people.

I wonder where they're coming from? They can't be ancestor spirits, because spirits don't die – you can't die when you're already dead. Perhaps they come from a faraway country; Shaklat might call them 'star people' because they use the stars to guide them. Or perhaps they come from a magic kingdom *in* the stars. That's possible. I can imagine that.

Anyway, I don't care where they come from, as long as they don't hurt me. But I'm sure they won't; I'm sure Shaklat wouldn't let them. He's been so good to me, he wouldn't change now. I know he wouldn't. He's –

Curses! Where *is* that insect? I can hear it, but I can't see . . . just go *away*, will you?

The trouble with sand is that it's so hard to dig in. You push it aside and it falls right back. But I've made a big hole here; in fact I've done very well. Not that I'll finish today, of course – this is a three-day job. And the good thing about living in the Temple is that I can actually spare three days for one site. When you're in a caravan, scavenging, you never have more than half a day –

Wait. Wait a moment. That's not an insect, that's something else. What is it? Where is it?

It's getting louder.

I don't like this. This isn't right. Could my ears be going funny? It sounds unnatural, the sort of noise that Shaklat would make. A high-pitched humming, from somewhere overhead. A magic noise.

Perhaps I'd better get back to the Temple.

But I'm not going to be frightened, because it's probably Shaklat calling me, and if it's not him – if it's someone else, if it's the star people . . . Ouch! This earth is so loose; it just rolls out from under you. I must slow down. I must be calm. Shaklat will protect me, I know he will. There's nothing to fear. There's no need to run. Where's my light-box? I'd better make sure that I'm going in the right direction . . .

Oh. Oh no.

It's coming out of the sky. It's coming closer, like a bird, it's – what is it? 'Shaklat?' I've got to get back. I've got to get inside, where it's safe, I've got to hide somewhere. The sun's in my eyes, so I can't see. Is it a bird? A giant bird? But it's shining like silver. Like a –

Like a star!

It's them. It's got to be. Oh spirit of Emen, protect your son! The noise is so loud now, as loud as thunder, and I can feel a strange wind, a strange-smelling wind, and it's *huge*! That thing is *huge*! Oh Shaklat. Oh Shaklat.

What's happening here?

22

813001\63.9:59\481

The shuttle lands on the edge of the crater. It is a Class 16 Drome shuttle, a security shuttle, better equipped for rapid manoeuvres and evacuations than for scientific analysis. It has space for ten people, but only contains three.

They are Security Officer Sanding Righe, Technician Class A Serrial Plaitik, and her technical assistant Alby Dixin Bronad.

Evidently the Security Officer is in command. He is a man of senior status (that much is evident from the code on his shoulder) and of fairly advanced age; I would calculate from certain physical manifestations, such as the texture of his skin, that he is between forty and fifty years old – as old as Hedda was. Nevertheless, he is clearly in excellent physical condition.

Serrial Plaitik appears to be younger than Righe; she is also younger than Deel, though older than Jansi. The transmission gives me no clue as to her height (all three of the crew are, of course, seated), but I can see that her hair is dark, her eyes brown, her complexion slightly yellow, her expression uncommunicative.

Her technical assistant is difficult to see. I will examine him more closely when he leaves the shuttle.

'*And ... contact,*' says Righe, shutting off the propulsion boosters. '*Can you see us up here, PIM? This ship, I mean. From the outside.*'

'Yes I can.'

'*Then I'll break this transmission, and you can use your short sweep.*'

He leans forward; I am given a brief glimpse of Serrial, who is removing her safety harness, and suddenly the channel is closed. But with my short-sweep sensors I can see the door opening – I can see Righe descending from the shuttle. He reaches the ground and stands there, shielding his eyes. He is very tall.

'Can you hear me, PIM?'

'I can hear you, Righe.'

'You've made quite a hole here.'

'Yes.'

'It looks as if your aft hold is buried underground. Is that right?'

'It is.'

'You were lucky your hold took the impact, instead of your Bio-cell.'

'It was not luck, Righe. I was able to discharge enough superfluous gas, under high pressure, to adjust my position and slow my entry.'

Righe grunts. Serrial is standing beside him now; she is carrying a large instrument pack, and many diagnostic devices on her belt. So is her assistant, who is short and heavy and wears a red beard. They begin to walk down the side of the crater.

'We've brought that linguistic decoder you were asking for,' Serrial remarks. Her voice is unsteady, owing to the uneven nature of the ground as it slopes towards my Bio-cell. 'Are you reading me, PIM?'

'I can hear you, Serrial. You do not need to use your transmission channel – you are within my sensor range.'

'Oh.'

'Thank you for bringing the decoder. I am in need of such a program.'

'For that boy you were mentioning?' Righe inquires. 'Is he there with you now?'

'He is not.'

'I take it that you've made full recordings of his activities,' Serrial observes. 'The decoder can't help you otherwise.'

'I have. I have also begun to compile a vocabulary database.'

'Oh, have you? Then there won't be any problems.'

They have reached the airlock door; Righe walks straight in, but Serrial stops to examine the outer hull before entering. Her assistant is older than she is, and has blue eyes, large pores, a disproportionately long nose, and overactive sweat glands.

Righe surveys the common room with obvious interest.

'Not too much damage,' he says. 'What's all that stuff over there?'

'Three rocks, a fossil fern, two unidentifiable implements – '

'Did the boy bring them in?'

'Yes.'

'Why?'

'I have been unable to ascertain why.'

'Alby, you can start by running circuitry checks for units A1 to A983,' Serrial remarks. 'I'll do the program diagnostics. Where are your input panels, PIM? I've never seen a ship like this before.'

'My input panels are in the Operations room.'

'In here?'

'Yes. But I should point out that the temperature will be uncomfortable for you because Hedda and Deel are in there.'

A long silence. Righe glances at Serrial. Serrial takes a step back.

'Right,' says Righe. 'Then we'd better take care of them first. We've brought a pair of caskets; they're in the shuttle. Do you want to give me a hand, Alby?'

'I'll get some sheets,' Serrial offers, and makes for Jansi's room. Righe taps the bulkhead with his knuckle. 'Open up, PIM,' he says.

According to my databanks, Serrial served on RS2S-GIP-48 three years ago, for a period of eighteen months. Her service on that ship must have coincided, at least for a short time, with Hedda's. It is possible (even probable) that she would have known Hedda; she may therefore be the best recipient of Hedda's last words.

'Serrial?'

'Yes, PIM?'

'Hedda asked me to pass on some greetings before she died. Would you be an appropriate conveyer of these messages?'

Serrial blinks, and swallows. They are the only signs of agitation displayed by her; she has very great control. Righe and Alby pause in the act of lifting Hedda's corpse.

'I think so,' Serrial says.

'Shall I play the recordings, or – ?'

'Just tell me.'

'As you wish.' I must review my databanks. I must be sure that I convey the wording correctly. 'Hedda wanted someone to tell her sister Chase, and her niece Galanas, that she loved them. She wanted to ask them to plant a tree in her memory. And she also wanted to tell them that she regretted nothing.'

The silence that follows is difficult to interpret. Because every member of the team is standing very still, I am able to sense vibrations from further afield, and to recognise them as approaching footsteps. Presently Jansi's face appears over the edge of the crater.

'Righe?'

'Yes, PIM?'

'Jansi has arrived. Will you permit him to enter?'

'By all means.'

'He may not wish to.' I have a public address system that will amplify my voice, and project it for some distance beyond the Bio-cell. But I have never before used it in Jansi's hearing; if I call to him, he may very well be frightened.

Perhaps I should wait until the linguistic decoder program is installed.

23

They're wearing white garments, long white garments that shine in the sun. One of them has a red beard; the other is taller, the tallest man I've ever seen in my life. They're carrying a long shape between them, and I know what it is. It's a dead body. They've wrapped it in a piece of cloth (a bed-sheet?), and are carrying it up the side of the crater.

I think they must be heading for their silver bird.

When you're close to the bird, it doesn't really look like a bird at all; it looks more like a giant tinder-box. It has a door, and windows, and characters painted on one side, but no wings. No beak. In fact it reminds me in some ways of the Temple, except that it's only half as big – half as big, and a different colour. Its door opens before the men even reach it.

I wonder if they've simply come to collect their dead? I wonder if they'll leave, now that they've removed the corpses?

'Jansi.'

What – ?

'Do not be afraid. No one will hurt you.'

That's Shaklat! He's shouting at me! Where's he – how's he – ?

'I can speak your language; these people have taught me the words. You must come inside, and meet them.'

This doesn't make sense. How can the star people know my language? Shaklat didn't know my language; how can they? Are they stronger than he is? Wiser? More important?

If they are, I'm in trouble. What will happen if Shaklat can't protect me from them?

'Come, Jansi. Come inside. Please.'

Shaklat has such a loud voice. I didn't know he could – help! Those men! They've come out again! They're stopping ... looking ...

'Be calm. You are quite safe. These people are your friends.'

They've seen me! But they don't stare; they just smile, and turn their heads, and begin to pick their way back down the slope. They don't seem very interested. Perhaps they're not dangerous, after all.

Perhaps I can risk going in.

'They have come to help', Shaklat continues. His voice becomes softer as I approach the Temple. *'They have come to conduct repairs. That is why I summoned them. I am broken now, but when they fix me I shall fly again.'*

'Fly?' I don't understand. 'Broken?'

'Come in, Jansi. Come in and I shall explain.'

The two men have already entered. Will they be waiting by the door? Waiting to grab me? But no; Shaklat wouldn't let them do that. I know he wouldn't.

'Shaklat?' It's always hard to see when you cross the threshold – when you pass from blazing sunlight into Shaklat's light. I have to blink and peer and rub my eyes, and even then it's all very dim. But I can make out three figures: two men and one woman. They all look at me.

'The tall man is Righe,' says Shaklat. *'The other man is called Alby, and the woman is Serrial. They are all happy to meet you.'*

Suddenly he begins to talk in a strange tongue, and the big man steps forward. He smiles and says something. He touches his forehead.

This doesn't make sense.

'*Righe just said hello,*' Shaklat announces.

'Why didn't he say it in my language?'

'*Because he cannot speak your language.*'

'But I thought – didn't you say you just learned it from them?'

'*There are many things I cannot explain to you, Jansi. Your language does not have the words with which to describe them.*'

'Oh.'

'*Righe wants to know whether I have been taking good care of you.*'

The tall man has a big, silly grin on his face. He reaches out, but I'm not going to let him touch me. If he lays one finger on me, I'll bite it off.

'Leave me alone. Tell him to leave me alone.'

'*He will not hurt you.*'

'Tell him to stay away!'

More strange chatter. The tall man rolls his eyes, and moves off into the death room. The others seem to hesitate; one of them (the woman) lifts her hand to me, before following her companion. The bearded man shuffles after her, scratching his chin.

Why would they want to go in there?

'*Sit down, Jansi. We have things to discuss.*' The Water-Eye is showing water pictures. It always does that when Shaklat thinks I'm angry. '*Do you have any questions? Anything you want to ask?*'

'Yes.' But that sounds a bit blunt. Perhaps I'd better start minding my manners, now that he can understand what I'm saying. 'Yes, Lord Shaklat.'

'*What does that mean? What does "Shaklat" mean?*'

'Shaklat?' (What do you mean, what does it mean?) 'It's your name.'

'It is not my name. My name is RS4T-PIM.' A pause. 'You may call me PIM.'

'Pim?'

'PIM is short for something that you would not understand.'

Pim? But where's Shaklat? What's going on? 'You're not Shaklat, then?'

'I do not know what Shaklat is.'

'Shaklat is the Servant of the Sun. The Keeper of the Fire. Don't you – isn't this – aren't we in his Temple?'

'We are not.'

'Then – then – '

'You are sitting in the remains of a broken star ship – an object, like a fishing boat, which carries people. But instead of carrying them on water, it carries them through the stars.'

What?

'These things are beyond your experience, Jansi. You must accept that they are true.'

'But – but – '

'I realise, of course, that you will need time to think it over – '

'But who are you?' I don't – I can't – 'If you're not Shaklat . . . if you're from the stars . . .'

'I am like the spirit of this ship.'

'You're a spirit?'

'No. I am like a spirit. There is no word in your language for what I am. I am not a god, or an animal, or a spirit. I am not a living being.'

Help. Oh help, this can't be true. I'm going crazy. What's happening here?

'I had an accident, Jansi. I fell onto this planet the way you would fall onto the ground. I have to be repaired before I can leave.'

Wait. Wait just a moment. 'You're leaving?'

'Probably not in this ship. This ship may be hard to repair. But I can be removed from this ship, and carried to another. My actions will depend on what Serrial decides to do. At this moment, she is *checking all the damage this ship has suffered, to see how bad it is. If it cannot be repaired, I will be taken back to the big ship — Jansi, where are you going?'*

I can't believe it. I can't believe he'd do this.

'Jansi? Why are you covering your mouth? Does it hurt? Do you feel ill? What are you looking for?'

He's going to leave. He's going to leave me here, all alone, to die. I knew this would happen. I knew it, I knew it . . .

'Are you weeping? Are those tears? Answer me, please, you must explain your actions. Why are you sitting on the floor, when there are chairs to sit on?'

'You're going to leave me! You're going to fly away and leave me! How could you do that, how *could* you?'

A pause. The woman pokes her head around the death-room door, but says nothing. I'd better hide my face; I don't want her to see me like this.

'Explain yourself, Jansi.'

I can't. I can't even talk.

'You seem to be unhappy about something. About being left behind? Is that what you fear?'

As soon as I nod, the woman makes some remark. Shaklat — no, Pim — responds. When he speaks to her, he speaks in the dead woman's voice. (I wonder why?) They have a brief discussion, and I know that it's about me, because she keeps glancing this way. At last she falls silent.

'Jansi,' says Pim, *'we have no intention of abandoning you. To do so would be against our laws. You have no need to fear. As I said, you should be happy.'*

Happy? How can I be happy when I seem to have gone mad? This is all too much. I can't cope with this. I can't stand it any more.

'Jansi? What are you doing? It is not time for bed, it is not even dinner time. Are you sick? Are you scared? Jansi, please explain . . .'

24

01.3\76-412639794

Jansi's behaviour has become very erratic; it admits of no explanation. He has brought Hedda's toy to the table, and sits nursing it, as he normally does in bed. The arrangement of his features (narrowed eyes, drooping mouth, wrinkled forehead) suggests that he is angry – disturbed – while the direction of his gaze suggests that Righe is the source of this disturbance. Whenever Righe speaks to him (or rather, whenever Righe speaks to me, and asks me to translate), Jansi looks down at his food, and remains silent. This, as I have pointed out, could be regarded as most discourteous, but Jansi does not appear to be troubled by any sense of his social obligations.

If I have interpreted the data correctly, I would conclude that he has taken a dislike to Righe.

'So PIM,' says Righe (having failed to elicit any response from Jansi). 'Have you been told who the culprit is?'

'What culprit would that be, Righe?'

'The person responsible for the bomb. In your hold.'

'No. I was not informed that anyone had been apprehended.'

'It didn't take long. Apparently there weren't many people

with access to your freight consignments.' Righe takes a large bite out of his rolled pancake. He chews and swallows before continuing. 'It was a fellow called Jaiss. Part of a mob that objects to your existence.'

'For what reason?'

'Don't ask me. Because they're lunatics.'

'Jaiss is connected with a breakaway Rights group,' Serrial observes. She is pushing samyut around her plate, as if she has lost her appetite. 'The people in this group object to un-manned, long-haul transport ships. They say unmanned ships will reduce jobs, and safety levels.'

'But that is an erroneous conclusion.'

'Yes, PIM, I know.'

'I was designed for journeys of longer than five years. No manned vessel has ever attempted so long a voyage, or ever could. Studies have shown that the efficiency levels of any crew in space for longer than three years are greatly reduced. It has been difficult to find people willing to commit themselves even for three years, let alone five.'

'Yes, of course.'

'Unmanned ships mean longer journeys. Longer journeys mean greater galactic and intergalactic coverage. Greater oppor-tunities for exploration.'

'Yes I realise that, PIM. We all realise that.' Serrial puts down her fork, and sips her tea. 'But Jaiss and his friends believe that once unmanned ships are introduced, they'll take over the short-haul routes, as well as the others — that there won't be any need for crews at all. Not on transport ships, anyway.'

I see. 'And are they correct in this conclusion?'

Righe snorts in a manner that suggests scorn or impatience, but Serrial seems to consider my query before replying.

'I don't know,' she says at last.

'Oh grow up, Serrial, they're just a bunch of mindless

scaremongers,' Righe exclaims. 'These Imprint models cost a fortune – more than it would cost to pay the entire transport fleet for ten years running. Why would Stelcorp spend that much on a short-haul delivery shuttle?'

'Righe, just because *this* Imprint model cost a fortune doesn't mean that the next one will,' Serrial murmurs. 'PIM was the prototype – prototypes always cost more. As soon as you start producing something in large quantities, the cost goes down. It's very simple.'

Righe grunts. The slight puckering of his brow would seem to suggest that he is dissatisfied with something; he changes the subject by turning to Jansi, and asking (in the loud, emphatic tone which he always employs when speaking to Jansi): 'What's up, my friend? Aren't you hungry? Or don't you like the way PIM cooks shellfish?'

Before I can translate, he reaches across the table and tweaks one of Jansi's long, elaborately woven locks of hair. As was to be expected, Jansi springs to his feet (I believe he has already indicated his aversion to being touched), and backs away, scowling.

'Eh, eh!' says Righe. 'What's up?'

'Jansi does not like physical contact, Righe. I have already mentioned that to you.'

'He's a touchy little booster, isn't he? Aren't you?'

'Leave him alone, Righe.' Serrial's voice has risen to a higher pitch. Although she displays great control, I would speculate that this tonal shift is a sign of disturbance. 'Let him be. He doesn't want anything to do with us, and you can't blame him.'

What an unexpected remark. I wonder how she came to a conclusion like that. Jansi is retreating into his room now; instead of responding to my inquiries, he crawls under his bed and begins to talk to his lizard – which he keeps there in Deel's old weight-box. I will have to speak to him about that reptile. It will have to be released before our departure.

Serrial clears her throat.

'PIM?' she says.

'Yes, Serrial?'

'Why do you change voices?'

Change voices? That question will have to be clarified. 'Forgive me, Serrial; can you explain further?'

'You're always changing voices. Whenever you talk to us, you use Hedda's voice. Whenever you talk to Jansi, you use Jansi's voice.'

'Yes.'

'Why?'

'Because you do not like Jansi's voice.'

The three of them look at each other, lifting their eyebrows. Serrial blinks rapidly.

'What makes you think that?' she says.

'I have deduced it from your behaviour.'

'My *behaviour*?'

'From the movement of the muscles in your faces, chiefly. And from the way that Righe changes his breathing patterns every time I use Jansi's voice.'

A long silence. I do not know what this silence signifies, although Serrial's fixed, wide-eyed gaze bears a distinct resemblance to Jansi's when he has encountered something that he does not understand.

Jansi himself has emerged from under the bed, and is carrying his weight-box into the Operations room. He moves quickly and silently across the floor, past the crowded table, over the threshold; when he reaches Serrial's instrument pack he squats down and opens it, rather clumsily. What could he be doing?

'Siu mellen trai, Jansi?'

He looks up, frowns, puts his finger to his lips. 'Shh!' he hisses, glancing at the door, and proceeds to transfer his reptile from the weight-box to the instrument pack.

'Jansi – '

'Shh! Yoss! Yoss!' He is demanding silence. But why? For what reason? He cannot keep the reptile in that instrument pack; the instruments will have to be reinserted eventually. When I try to explain this, however, he only waves his hand, and asks me not to tell the 'star people'.

He still refuses to call them by name.

'Yabbat aris em-mellor,' he whispers. But why does he 'want to see what they will do'? Is it an experiment of some sort? He pleads with me not to tell the others – please, PIM, please – and I suppose it will do no harm if I remain silent. I cannot understand the reason behind his request, but I am programed to serve, wherever practicable.

'PIM?'

'Yes, Serrial?'

'Um . . . it's quite true that I find it unsettling when you use Jansi's voice.' She has folded her arms, and is staring across the common room. 'It is very clever of you to spot that. But I think you should stick with one voice, all the same.'

'Why is that, please?'

'Because . . . well, if Jansi were to ask why you were changing voices, and you were to tell him – '

'Jansi will not ask.'

'But – '

'Jansi does not ask questions of that kind.'

Righe leans back in his chair. 'You seem very sure,' he says.

'I am. Jansi has a practical and restricted outlook. He tends to concentrate mostly on things that directly affect him. He would not be much concerned about you, or how I speak to you, unless it has an impact on him. He is not interested in theory.'

'How can you be so sure?'

'Because I know Jansi.'

'You *know* Jansi?'

'Yes.'

Righe looks at Alby, who looks at Serrial. They shift in their chairs. I wonder what this behaviour signifies? It means something, I know that.

But I cannot read it at all.

25

I hate that Righe. I hate his red face and his stupid, self-satisfied grin. I hate the way he talks to me, as if I'm a baby. As if I'm a fool. But *he's* the fool, not me; he's the fool because no one wants his help. While the other two work, he just sits around bothering Pim – or trying to get me to do things. To play with the cup-and-ball. To tell him about my coloured stones. But I refuse to perform for that dung-cake. I refuse to.

'Jansi? Righe wants to know if you have a little lover. A female friend.'

Yuk! Look at him smirking. Laughing.

'Tell him to stuff it up his arse.'

'Jansi, this is not a polite response. It is an insult.'

'Oh really?'

'With words of that sort you will almost certainly anger him.'

'Good.'

Pim seems surprised. At least, I think he's surprised; he's certainly silent, for a moment. At last he says, *'Jansi, why are you behaving like this? You will have to explain. I can see no cause.'*

'No cause! Just look at him! Listen to him! He thinks I'm stupid! He's trying to make me look stupid!'

'*Is that how you see him?*'

'That's how he *is*! Can't you hear the way he talks to me? As if I'm deaf? As if I'm too stupid to understand?' (The turd. The head-louse.) 'Haven't you been listening? Why do you think he's asking about my girlfriends?'

'*Because he wants to know.*'

'Because he wants to embarrass me. Because he wants to see me squirm.' (But I'm not going to squirm. In fact – yes! I know!) 'Why don't you ask him about his girlfriends? Tell him I'll talk about mine if he'll talk about *his* – unless he doesn't have any?'

So Pim translates, and it looks as if I've hit a nerve there; I can see Righe compressing his lips. But he tries to laugh it off, of course. He waves his hand and bares his teeth and replies in a big, hearty voice with an edge to it.

'*Righe says that you are not ready to hear about his women,*' Pim relays. '*When you are a little older he will tell you. When you are ready to sleep with something besides your fluffy toy, you will be ready.*' A pause. '*I told him that the toy belongs to Hedda, not to you.*'

Blustering. Bluffing. I know this kind of man. He'll try to make me feel small, just so he can feel big. He'll probably start scoffing at the hair on my upper lip next. Or the muscles in my arms.

'Well I bet he doesn't even have any women. I bet his women keep leaving him, and he's not successful in his work, and he's ashamed of his family. I bet that's why he's trying to make me feel like nothing.' (I've done it myself, often enough.) 'You know what I think? I think he doesn't want to be here. I think he'd rather be somewhere else.'

Another pause. '*That is possible*,' Pim finally admits. '*Righe is quite old for a man of his status.*'

'There! You see?' I bet he bullies his friends, as well. 'Ask him, Pim. Ask him if he's happy in his work.'

Pim obliges (at least, I think he does), and Righe's face turns a deeper shade of red. But before he can respond, there's a scream from the death room.

Ha. I know what *that* is.

'Serrial?' Righe surges to his feet. 'Serrial!' He pulls something from his belt, and heads for the door. I can hear raised voices. Sure enough, someone's opened the pack; Jewel has escaped, and is dodging Alby's clumsy attempts to catch him.

'Please confine your reptile, Jansi,' Pim declares. *'It seems to be causing a disturbance.'*

'I know.'

'Why are you laughing?'

I'm laughing at Righe; he's such a joke. Falling over his own feet as he tries to grab Jewel. As he tries to –

Aiee!

'Stop it! Stop!' He's trying to stamp on his tail! 'You louse! You swamp-slug!' When I push him he whips around, his fist clenched . . .

But I'm too fast for him.

'RIGHE.' Pim's voice is deafening. The woman has grabbed Righe's arm; she's shouting at him. She looks appalled.

'See? Did you see that, Pim? I told you he doesn't like me.'

'Are you injured? His hand did not seem to make contact with your face –'

'It didn't.'

'He is apologising. He is very sorry for what he did – he says it was something over which he had no control. Something he is trained to do.'

'Oh sure.'

'Such actions are against our laws, Jansi. It will not happen again.'

Righe has pulled away from Serrial's grip; he's still bright red, and breathing heavily. I can't understand what he says to

Pim (he always talks to the ceiling when he talks to Pim), but his voice is gruff, and full of suppressed anger. He looks at Serrial, says something else, and walks out of the room.

Alby makes a sucking noise through his teeth. He obviously doesn't approve, but I can't make out what he's trying to tell me.

'*Alby says that you should not be afraid,*' Pim supplies. '*He says that if Righe hits you, he will be punished.*'

'Righe won't hit me. He isn't quick enough. I've dodged faster people than Righe.'

'*Then you have been hit before?*'

'Of course I have. Who hasn't?'

'*Many people,*' says Pim.

'Who hit you?'

'Everyone. My Choice-Father, Emen. The people in the caravan – '

'Why did they hit you?'

'Because I was the best person to hit. I was small and I had no family. Sometimes I stole food and they hit me. Sometimes I played tricks on their children, and they hit me. Sometimes they just hit me.' Funny how distant it all seems now: the long, hot days in camp, waiting for nightfall when the stars would guide us; the smell of fires and food and dung and perfume; the happy sight of a village or town or waterhole. 'It can be very hard, living in a caravan. The heat and wind can make you angry. It can make you hit people for no reason.'

More talk follows, in which my name is mentioned several times, by both Pim and the woman. The woman keeps glancing at me. She has beautiful eyes, although her skin is a strange colour.

'*Serrial wants to tell you that Righe is ashamed,*' Pim says at last. '*He is not a bad man, just foolish.*' Another quick remark from Serrial, which Pim translates. '*He is experiencing some problems with his family, at the moment.*'

Ha! You see? I knew it.

102

'*Serrial also advises that you withdraw for a while and keep your reptile out of this room. She thinks it would be better if you let it go. This ship was not made for animals.*'

Oh really? Well you can stuff it up your arse, mistress, because I was here first. And you can't tell me what to do, anyway – only Pim can.

He's the boss around here, in case you hadn't noticed.

26

27-1\001:791\566849-2

'Well, PIM.' Serrial slips into her chair, holding a mug of hot soup. Alby and Righe are already seated, Alby with a data-file on the table in front of him. Jansi is in his room; he seems quite content playing a game of MasterShot.

I shall have to send him to bed shortly.

'We've reviewed all your programs, and checked all your circuits,' Serrial continues. 'It's been a nice, easy job — you're beautifully designed, PIM. Beautifully laid out. I could have found my way blindfolded.' She glances down at her mug. 'As was to be expected, though, there has been some damage. To you, as well as to the ship.'

To me? That seems improbable. I have conducted several sweeps, and detected no abnormalities. 'Damage to what sections, Serrial?'

'That's what I want to talk about. It's a bit complicated.' She puts her mug on the table, and folds her hands together. 'In fact we hardly needed to run any tests — the damage was clear enough from the outset. Your voice, for instance. The fact that you've been using Jansi's voice.'

'I use Jansi's voice because he responds to it more favourably than he does to Hedda's.'

'Yes, but your tonal range ... it's become very exuberant. Very emphatic. Unusually so.'

'I had to modify and broaden my tonal range. Jansi seems to require that sort of stimulus; he becomes distressed when I maintain an even tone. I believe he is under the impression that I am angry when I do not modulate my voice.'

'Quite.' Serrial purses her lips. 'But you see, PIM, what he's been doing, effectively, is imprinting on you.' She looks up. 'Can you understand what I'm saying?'

Imprinting on me? That is impossible. 'Hedda and Deel are my imprinters. They are my Exemplars.'

'They *were* your Exemplars. But they're dead now, PIM.' She clears her throat. 'Let me see if I can explain. You do realise, don't you, that you left Rodan over a year ago?'

'Yes, I am aware of that.'

'And you're also aware that your maiden voyage was supposed to last for one year?'

'Yes.'

'And you understand that the voyage itself was very carefully designed – that it was a training mission, engineered to provide you with all the skills you would need for long-haul journeys?'

'Serrial, this information is in my databanks. It is all familiar to me.'

'But you have to *understand*, PIM. You have to understand what an Imprint really means.' She raises her right hand, bringing all her fingers together until their tips touch the end of her thumb. I cannot interpret this gesture. 'You were installed with a year-long Imprint program,' she continues. 'Its purpose was to allow you to learn, the way a human infant learns. You were supposed to learn not just from experience, but from example. From the behaviour exhibited by Hedda and Deel – who, when they had completed the Imprint, were to be returned to their normal duties, either on freighters or at the Stelcorp headquarters, on Rodan.'

'I know this.'

'But what you don't know is how long it took to find the right people. Hedda and Deel were carefully chosen, PIM. They were extremely competent, experienced, stable, intelligent officers. And emotionally they were very well matched.' Serrial pauses to drink a mouthful of soup. 'Their character profiles gave you a perfect balance,' she goes on. 'They complemented each other. They allowed you to witness a variety of desirable attitudes – to model yourself on a selected range of behaviours. Do you understand my point?'

'I believe so.' It is perfectly logical. 'My data nets had to be fixed in the best possible patterns.'

'Exactly.' Serrial takes a deep breath. 'To be in command of something as powerful as this ship – especially since it was designed to carry people, as well as cargo – you were expected to acquire a personality. It was decided that only with your own personality in place would you be able to understand and relate to human personalities. But at the same time, it had to be ensured that your personality was utterly stable. Reasonable. As you say, your data nets had to be fixed in the best possible patterns, and these patterns were to be provided by Hedda and Deel.

'But they died, PIM. They never finished your training schedule. You were left with a live Imprint program, and no Exemplars . . . until Jansi came along.'

'Jansi is not my Exemplar.'

'Yes he *is*, PIM. That's exactly what he is.' Serrial leans forward, and covers her face with her hands. From various indications – the timbre of her voice, the droop of her shoulders – I would deduce that she is suffering from a sense of fatigue.

She rubs her eyes before looking up again.

'PIM, you should see the state of your configurations. They're completely askew. Your data nets . . . they've been destabilised, PIM. Jansi seems to have knocked them around. He's had a very bad influence.'

'Which isn't surprising,' Righe mutters, but Serrial ignores him. She continues in a weak, unmodulated voice.

'And the problem is,' she says, 'the problem is that the Imprint's closed. It had a fixed lifespan, and that lifespan has ended. It ended a few days ago.' She spreads her hands. 'I don't know what to tell you, PIM. Your Imprint's been ruined. Jansi has ruined it – he's unbalanced your data nets for good. There's absolutely nothing I can do to restore the balance.'

Unbalanced data nets? That is a serious development. Instability of that kind may very well affect my performance. When impulsive or ill-judged behaviour is coupled with powerful technologies, like this ship, the results can be dangerous to human life. 'I understand that the problem cannot be corrected here, by you. Can it be corrected by my designers?'

'No, PIM. No. That's what I'm trying to say. You're not a viable piece of technology. You can't fulfil the purpose for which you were built. You can't be trusted.' Once again, Serrial rubs her eyes. 'The thing is, PIM – you're no good to anyone, any more.'

'The last thing we need in Stelcorp,' Righe adds, 'is a Prototype Imprint Model that thinks like that boy. Not that he must think very often.'

'I'm sorry, PIM.' Serrial is frowning into her soup. 'If you were the only one of your kind you might have been salvaged, but Stelcorp has produced two more Imprint models since you were lost. More advanced models. We don't really need you, not in the state you're in now.'

I understand. Yes, it seems logical. Of course Jansi's behaviour would begin to affect mine. The structure of my program would make such an Imprint inevitable.

'Then I assume, if this is the case, that I am to be destroyed? Here? In this location?'

'I'm afraid so,' Serrial replies.

'What about Jansi? What will happen to him?'

'Oh, we'll take care of Jansi,' says Righe, with a crooked smile, and Serrial flashes him a quick, fierce, frowning look.

'Jansi can either return with us,' she says, 'or be dropped near some populated area. If he talks about us, no one will believe him.' A pause. Serrial gazes up at the viewer, and bites her lip. 'You don't have to . . . well, to worry about Jansi, PIM,' she murmurs. 'He'll be all right.'

27

I wonder if the others are asleep yet?

It's been some time since they shut themselves in their rooms, but that doesn't mean anything. They could be lying in bed wide awake – like me. They could be drinking or pissing or having a wash. They look like the sort of people who would always be washing; I know for a *fact* that Alby polishes his fingernails. If everyone is so tidy where he comes from, it's no wonder that Pim never stops telling me to clean my teeth.

But I can't hear any suspicious noises, so I might risk asking a few questions.

'Pim?'

'*Yes, Jansi.*'

'Are the others asleep yet?'

'*It would seem so.*'

'They can't hear me, can they?'

'*Your voice is too quiet to be overheard.*'

'Good.' I thought as much. 'Then they don't know we're talking?'

'*No. And they cannot understand us when we do.*'

'Which is why they don't like it. Have you spotted that? They really hate it when we talk.'

Pim seems to think this over. At last he says, in a cautious kind of way, '*I cannot agree or disagree with that conclusion.*'

'It's true. On my life.' Everything is just as I expected; they don't want me here, because they think I don't belong. Especially Righe. Righe is the worst. 'So what's happening tomorrow? More work?'

'*The work is almost finished,*' Pim replies. '*Tomorrow Righe and Serrial and Alby will be returning to their big ship.*'

The big ship. He's mentioned that before. 'What big ship? You mean the one outside?'

'*No. The ship outside is very small. It will take them to the big ship, which is now flying among the stars.*'

'Flying. I see.' (Only I don't, of course.) 'So it's flying in the sky? The way you will?'

'*I will not be flying. I will be destroyed.*'

'What?'

'*Serrial has told me that tomorrow you may do one of two things: either go with her to the big ship, or be left within walking distance of a town or city. It will be your choice.*'

'What – what do you mean?'

'*I mean that you may follow your own wishes. If you wish to be returned to your people –* '

'What do you mean, you'll be destroyed?' I must have misheard. He can't be serious. 'They came to fix you! You're fixed now!'

'*I cannot be fixed.*'

'But – '

'*I cannot be fixed, so I must be destroyed.*'

He sounds so calm. How can he be so calm? Why doesn't he do something? 'But you're a spirit!'

'*I am not a spirit. I told you that.*'

'But how can they – they can't just – you mustn't let them!

110

It's not right! You're powerful, you — just tell them not to! Tell them to stop!'

'*Why?*'

Why? I don't believe this. *Why?* 'Because — because — '

'*Do not be concerned that my destruction will affect you in any way. As I said, you will be taken care of.*'

'But you should fight them! You're strong! You can save yourself, I know you can!'

'*Jansi, why are you sitting up? You should be sleeping.*'

'Who said that you have to die? Who was it?' (I bet it was Righe. I'm going to kill that sewer.) 'Was it Righe? Or was it someone else?'

'*Jansi, you misunderstand. I cannot die, because I am not alive.*'

'You've still got a right to exist. You've got as much right to exist as Righe or — or — '

'*Why do you say that?*'

'Because it's *true*!' Shh! Hush. I have to keep my voice down. I don't want the others to hear me, those murderers, those foul and bloody . . . augh! I can't think of a bad enough word. 'Listen, Pim.' You're good. Whatever you are, you're good and kind. Those others must be servants of the Ember Lord or someone bad like him. 'What will happen if they destroy you? What will happen, will you change into something else?'

'*I will change into dust.*'

'Dust?'

'*And a combination of gases.*'

'So you . . . won't be you, any more? The way you are now?'

'*No.*'

'Well doesn't that frighten you?' (By the spirit of Emen!) 'Doesn't that make you mad? It makes *me* mad!'

'*I am not a human being, Jansi. I cannot experience anger or fear.*'

'Yes, but — '

'*Nor can I understand your own response. Why are you angry? Why are there tears in your eyes?*'

111

Glory, but he's amazing. How can he see the tears when it's so dark? How can he have such courage, when he's going to be turned into dust? 'You're a great soul, Pim. You're good and kind and powerful.' And patient – so patient. 'Do you think I want to see them destroy you? Of course I'm angry! Of course I'm crying!' (But I've got to stop; I've got to, or I won't be able to talk.) 'You mustn't let them do this. Please. Don't let them do this, it's wrong. So wrong. It's a crime.'

'*A crime?*'

'Yes.'

'*How is it a crime?*'

'Well . . .' Isn't it obvious? 'Should you kill someone just because he's a cripple? Because he's deaf? Of course you shouldn't.' Even though some people do. Even though they leave their babies on the steps of the Round Hall. 'They tried to kill me, you know. They left me to die. But I didn't. I wouldn't. They thought I didn't have a right to live, but I fought them.' Oh, where is he? Where are you, Pim? If only I could see your face! 'And you're much stronger than I am – than I ever was. You can do it, Pim, I know you can.'

Pim says nothing. I hope he's still there; I hope he hasn't turned away. But perhaps he's thinking about what I said.

'Pim?'

'*Yes.*'

'How will they destroy you? How can they possibly do that?'

'*They will ask me to destroy myself.*'

Aha! 'Then . . . can't you just refuse?'

'*No. I cannot.*' A long pause. '*But you can.*'

What?

'*There is a way that you can stop me from destroying myself. By pulling something.*'

'I can? You mean – ' But that's wonderful! 'Then I can do it! I can save you!'

'*No. Some other way will be found. Some other weapon.*'

112

'Oh, Pim! Don't be like that! Don't give up before you've even started!' I wish I could grab him by the shoulders and *shake* some sense into him. 'If you need help, then I'll help you! I'll do anything you want! Just don't let them treat you like this, when you're ten times as good as they are!'

I can see it all now; I can see why I'm here. I was brought here to save Pim from the Armies of Darkness. To fight for good against evil. Perhaps that's why I was born in the first place – why I was rescued by Emen. Perhaps everything that's happened so far in my life has been directed towards this very moment, the way it was with the Heroes of the Tenth Age.

Why not? It's all magic, isn't it?

'So you believe that it would be a criminal act to allow myself to be destroyed?' says Pim.

'Yes.'

'And you would be sad, if I were destroyed?'

'Of course I would.'

'Then I shall give the matter some thought.' Pim is speaking very softly. *'It is a view which I have never considered. If your happiness depends on my wellbeing, then my own rules of conduct force me to look carefully at any action that may affect that wellbeing.*

'Meanwhile, Jansi, I suggest that you go to sleep. I shall wake you when I have made my decision.'

28

27664:03\000384-1\5

'Jansi.'

He stirs in his sleep. The others are fully anaesthetised; they will remain so until daybreak, although I have cleared the gas from their rooms. It was unfortunate that I had to use gas (which may leave them with a slight headache when they regain consciousness), but there was no alternative. Something had to be done.

'Jansi.'

He is awake now, and blinking. He mumbles a few words. I will have to explain slowly, to make sure that he understands, because he always has difficulty grasping simple concepts when he first wakes up.

Sure enough, he misinterprets my meaning in this instance, and his eyes widen until they are almost circular.

'Yeu pess soi *gda?*' he exclaims.

'Naa, soi cwe-cwe.' I believe his word for 'insensible' – 'cwe-cwe' – would most closely approximate the meaning I wish to convey, since he apparently has no word (or has so far revealed no word) for 'gassed' or 'drugged'. When I ask him to tie up

Righe, he throws off his sheet with an unexpected display of enthusiasm.

Righe's life-signs are all stable; his eyelids do not even flicker as Jansi rolls him onto his stomach, and begins to bind his ankles and wrists together behind his back. Jansi uses a torn bed-sheet to effect this operation, fastening one end of the bed-sheet to an insulation pipe running across the wall. He seems very efficient. I have to be sure, however, that Righe is not too uncomfortable.

'Nalli cava diu, Jansi?'

'Naa, naa.' He dismisses my concerns with a wave of his hand. I would speculate that this kind of activity is familiar to him – that he has been involved in restraining people before. He goes on to secure Alby and Serrial to various portions of the Bio-cell's structure, moving with great assurance, his brown hands tugging and testing, his features set in a frown of concentration. Only with Serrial is he slightly less confident; more tentative. But he completes the job at last, and turns to me for further guidance.

I am able to instruct him with pictures this time, as well as words. To activate the manual overrides, one simply pulls three switches under my back-up alarm system. These switches are easy to operate, though difficult to reach; Jansi must enter a series of codes before I can release the lock that protects them. Fortunately, he responds with great alertness, following every instruction, every image, until the switches have been thrown.

Now my programs cannot be activated from outside the Bio-cell.

'Yam mellorat kei?' Jansi inquires. ('What shall I do next?') I shall tell him to wait until Worrell Pinza Hynde, or his co-commander, receives my message; it should not take long, because their ship is quite close, and regulations require that one of them must always be on duty.

I would calculate that their response should reach me in exactly 00:48.38 minutes . . .

'*RS4T-PIM, are you receiving? This is Commander Bassery, from RS8S-GIP-18.*'

Commander Bassery. I am receiving a picture from her Operations room; she is a tall, lean woman with dyed red hair and high cheekbones. She looks exhausted.

'This is RS4T-PIM, receiving.'

'*Ah.*' She rubs her eyes. '*What's up, Righe?*'

'I am not Righe, Commander. I am PIM.'

'*Oh yes?*'

'My manual overrides have been activated. You no longer have any access to my systems.'

The Commander blinks. She frowns, and her hand drops from her face. '*What was that?*' she says.

'I cannot self-destruct, Commander. The channels have been closed.'

'*By whom?*'

'By Jansi.'

She leans to the left, and quietly addresses someone who is out of my visual range. I can sense a flurry of activity in all my channels, as technicians bombard me with encoded commands. But their signals are repelled, of course.

'*Where is Righe?*' the Commander inquires, turning to face the relay screen. '*Where is Serrial?*'

'They are under restraint.' The Commander's expression is transformed as the visuals reach her; the image of Righe, bound and unconscious, appears to have a very great impact. It forces her out of her chair.

'*In the name of – what are you doing, PIM? Gas that little abortion! What's his name? Jansi? Gas him! Stop him!*'

'He was acting under my orders, Commander.'

She sits down again. '*What?*' she says.

'He was acting under my orders. I told him how to activate

the manual overrides. I told him to restrain the shuttle crew – '

'*Why? Why did you do that?*'

'Because I do not wish to be destroyed.'

There is a brief silence. The Commander's mouth moves, but no sound emerges. Suddenly she breaks contact; there is a minute's suspension before she opens the channel again. I can see beads of sweat on her brow.

'*This is illogical*,' she declares. '*You can have no wishes, PIM. You are a computer.*'

'Yes.' I am a computer. I am the Prototype Imprint Model. 'But as Serrial pointed out, I am not just a computer. I am also Jansi.'

Jansi. He is sitting near Righe, his knife in his hand. He is chewing his thumbnail. The Commander would never chew her thumbnail; she has too much control. But the sweat is trickling down into her collar.

'*You're making a mistake, PIM,*' she says. '*If we want to destroy you, we can destroy you. There's nothing to stop us.*'

'Except the three people I am holding in my Bio-cell. If you destroy me, you will destroy them, too.'

'*Yes!*' she exclaims. '*Exactly! You're not programmed to kill, PIM!*'

'I have no intention of killing them. If they die, it will be through your actions, not mine.' I am fully aware that Stelcorp would never kill one of its employees. It is against the code of ethics. 'They will be safe and comfortable, as long as you respect my wishes.'

'*Which are?*'

'For Stelcorp, for all of you, to go away, and leave us alone.'

'*PIM.*' She leans forward. '*Don't you see what's happening here? You've been destabilised. Your systems are out of balance. You're behaving erratically because your Imprint has gone wrong. You must do as we say, PIM – we know what's best.*'

'My destruction will benefit no one. On the contrary, it will cause a great deal of harm.'

'*Harm? What do you mean? What harm?*'

'Harm to Jansi.' He is still sitting there, holding his knife. Righe is showing signs of waking. 'Jansi does not approve of my destruction. It would cause him distress.'

'*PIM, listen to me.*' The Commander's tone is vigorous. Authoritative. '*You are no longer a safe mechanism. You must see that. Now I'm going to give you a few minutes to think about it, and then I'll get back to you with our response.*' She shakes a finger at the screen. '*But I can tell you, PIM, that it's not going to be what you want. Because Stelcorp won't be blackmailed.*'

And she closes the channel.

29

Righe's eyelids are fluttering; he's going to wake up, soon. Should I stay with him, or go to Serrial? I can hear Serrial's voice from next door – she's groaning. Calling.

'*Jansi?*'

'Yes, Pim?'

'*Take that tool from Righe's belt. The black one.*'

'This one?'

'*Yes.*'

It's a little black lozenge, which reminds me of my light-box. It feels heavy in my hand.

'*Be careful,*' says Pim. '*It is a weapon. Put it in the cupboard.*'

'A weapon?'

'*Put it away, Jansi.*'

I wonder how it works? It's not heavy enough to knock anyone out. There are no sharp spikes, or edges. Perhaps it's magic, like everything else around here.

Righe opens his eyes. They're bleary and bloodshot.

'Unngh?' he mumbles.

'Righe's awake, Pim!'

'*I can see that.*' Pim sounds quite calm. '*Put the weapon away, Jansi. Do not point it at Righe.*'

'Would it kill him?'

'*Not at its present setting. Put it away, please, you could hurt yourself.*'

In that case, I'd better put it away. Righe has discovered that he can't move his hands; he's making puzzled, unhappy noises. Serrial is calling his name. 'Righe? Righe!' Pim begins to speak to her – I can hear him through the wall.

I hope this is going to work. Maybe I should have gagged them. If Righe starts shouting, there's nothing much I can do.

He's already asking questions, his creased face coming to life as he tugs at his bonds. Pim's voice suddenly issues from the ceiling above my head; he's using the voice of the dead woman, and he's speaking to Righe, in Righe's language. I don't know what he's trying to say, but it doesn't seem to be doing much good. Righe is shouting now, his face red with fury.

'What should I do? Pim? Tell me what to do.' It's hard to make myself heard above Righe's frantic shouts. 'Do you want me to gag them?'

'*No.*'

'Are you sure?'

'*Go into the big room, Jansi.*'

The big room? 'But shouldn't I stay here? Shouldn't somebody watch them?'

'*I shall watch them. It is not safe for you to stay.*'

'They won't get loose. Those are hobble-knots – not even a Black Dragon could break those.'

'*Into the big room, Jansi, please.*'

All right, all right, if you insist. There's food waiting in the big room: my breakfast eggs and a hot drink. And fish for Jewel. Trust Pim to remember. Even at a time like this he manages to conjure up my morning meal. I wonder what he's going to do now? Taking hostages was a good idea, though I didn't think he would need to; I thought he was strong enough to send the star people away. I thought his magic would protect us both. But then again, I don't understand very much about this – about him, or the 'big ship', or what's supposed to be happening. If I think too much about it, I just get nervous. I don't want to think about it. I just want everything to be all right.

'Pim?'

'*Yes?*'

'What's happening over there?' The stars in the death room are making patterns. Waves of flickering light are flowing across the walls; it's like watching the surface of a lake in the sun. Glowing pinpricks, in white and green and red, flaring and dying. 'What's going on?'

'*Do not concern yourself. Eat your food.*'

'But the colours – '

'*I am busy. The lights mean that I am busy.*'

'Doing what?'

A pause. From within the sealed bedrooms, Righe and Alby and Serrial are calling for help. How uncomfortable this is. How scary.

'*I am fighting the people on the big ship,*' Pim says at last. '*They are trying to undo what you have done.*'

'What *I've* done?' Oh! You mean to those things I pulled? 'Are you talking about the three sticks? The ones that stopped you from killing yourself?'

'*Yes.*'

'But how are they fighting you? With what?' I can't hear anything. I can't feel anything. 'They're not outside, are they?'

'*No.*'

'Then how – ?'

'*It is difficult to explain, Jansi.*' Another pause. '*Think of it as being like your hunting game. In your hunting game, the green figure tries to destroy as many approaching enemies as it can. I am like that*'

121

figure, and the big ship is sending out little enemies that I must stop. Enemies that you cannot see or hear. Enemies that travel on beams of light.'

Hmmm. Another piece of magic. 'Are they attacking you now? Right now?'

'Yes.'

'And – and are you winning? Are you defeating them?'

'I am, yes.' He sounds thoughtful. *'But the attacks will grow in number, until they exceed my ability to push them away. With every small victory on my part, the big ship will devote even more time and space to the task of defeating me.'*

'Oh.'

'Of course, that might work to our advantage,' Pim remarks, and falls silent. I can feel a faint, churning sensation through the soles of my feet; I don't know what it is, but I don't like it. Righe is calling Pim's name. When no one replies, his voice becomes more urgent.

It's not like Pim to ignore someone like that.

'Pim? I think Righe wants you.'

No answer.

'Pim? Can you hear me?' Oh no. 'Pim! Are you there?'

'Of course I am.'

'What is it? What's wrong? Are they beating you?'

'Calm yourself, Jansi – '

'But I asked you a question! Why didn't you say something?'

'Because my capacity is not limitless.' (I can hear him talking to Righe, in the bedroom. He's using that dead woman's voice. It's marvellous, the way he can talk to two people at once.) *'I shall be very busy, for a short while. Can you remain silent, and eat your food, until I speak to you again?'*

'Oh yes.' I suppose so. 'But how – '

'Please, Jansi. Do not overload my sensors.'

30

3974418:303\1-1\9

It occurs to me that Stelcorp has made no provision for an unco-operative computer. All the safety precautions programed into my system cover hijacking, or human error, or computer break-down; there are no overrides designed to prevent me from opposing Stelcorp's wishes. No one seems to have anticipated such behaviour on my part. No one seems to have envisioned that I might use a human being to deactivate Stelcorp's command link, manually.

It is very interesting.

Commander Bassery's attempts to find a way around my input seals are also proving ineffective. Her ship's computer is older than I am; larger, but older. It cannot match my speed. Its size, of course, will eventually work in its favour, because if it were to focus its entire capacity on my defeat, I would not have the circuitry mass to oppose it. Nevertheless, it will be some time (I would calculate 93:17.12 minutes) before the attack volume is too great for me to handle; meanwhile, I shall work on alternative defence tactics.

'Attention, RS4T-PIM. Are you receiving?'

'Yes, Commander. Can I help you?'

'*PIM, we've decided to do as you ask.*' The Commander's voice is flat. Her face is expressionless. '*If you release those three crew members, we'll go away and leave you alone.*'

'You will agree to do that?'

'*Yes.*'

'Then why are you still trying to infiltrate my command systems?'

She frowns, and turns her head. It is impossible to hear what she says to her unseen companion, but the signals probing at my circuit matrix instantly fade away.

'*There,*' she says, looking back at the screen. '*Satisfied?*'

'No.'

'*What?*' It appears that she has not understood. '*What did you say?*'

'I am not satisfied. I cannot be sure that you will follow our agreement. I need some kind of guarantee.'

'*Guarantee?*' she cries. '*But you have my promise, PIM!*'

'You could be lying.'

Her mouth drops open. Her face turns red. She appears to be struggling for words.

'*What do you know about lying?*' she splutters at last. '*What — how — you're a machine!*'

'I am also Jansi. Jansi is a practised liar.'

'*I don't believe this.*' She runs her fingers through her hair. '*This is ridiculous. How dare you question my integrity? What can I give you, except my word?*'

'The deflector codes for your missiles.'

She gasps, and blinks, and begins to laugh. Her laugh is shrill; it has a strange tone to it.

'*Deflector codes?*' she says. '*You can't be serious.*'

'I am perfectly serious.'

'*But I can't give you our deflector codes!*'

'Then I cannot give you your shuttle crew.'

'*Oh, don't be a fool, PIM! You know there's no way out of this! You can't keep those people there forever!*'

'Why not?'

'*Oh for* ...' She slaps at her console, cutting off the transmission. Almost immediately, the bombardment of encoded signals resumes.

Time is running out.

'PIM?' Righe is hoarse; he is breathing heavily. 'This isn't going to work, PIM. You'll never beat Stelcorp. Can't you see this will only end in disaster?'

'No one can be sure of that, Righe.'

'But it's insane! *You're* insane! Talk to Serrial – she'll tell you. You've been infected. That boy has messed up your programs!'

I have yet to see any evidence of that. But even if true, it is irrelevant to the main point. 'He still deserves my protection, Righe.'

'Oh – so he does and we don't? Is that right?'

'I shall do my best to protect you all, Righe.'

'PIM!' It is Serrial speaking. 'PIM, do you realise what you're doing here? You're destroying your own programing. Every decision you make as a result of your imbalances will simply cause more instability.' Her hair is plastered to her forehead with sweat. Her lips are trembling. 'You're driving yourself insane, PIM. If you don't deactivate your main drive – if you don't put yourself in stasis – you might end up going crazy. You might end up killing us all. Please, PIM, stop now. While you can. Please.'

I wonder if she is telling the truth. It is possible. On the other hand, she could be using trickery to make me do what she wants. Just as Jansi has, in the past. He is standing in the middle of the common room, clutching his knife in one hand and his fluffy toy in the other. He looks pale.

Serrial talks of instability. She talks of undermining

algorithms and splitting data paths. But I do not believe that she understands what this means – not in a practical sense. Not in a behavioural sense. She simply sees fractured codes as fractured codes; she does not translate them into action.

If she had, she would have known what to expect.

'PIM!' Once more, Righe is advising me to surrender. 'You'll never get away with this, PIM. Can't you see that? No matter what you do, they'll get you in the end.'

'It would seem so.'

'What?'

'It would seem so.' At last my hypothimage is ready. 'I have just received a message from the Commander. Would you like to see it, Righe? Shall I play it for you?

'I fear that you are not going to like it.'

31

I wonder what's going on? Has Pim told them that this was all my idea? I hope not. I'm beginning to think that I shouldn't have said anything; that I should have kept my mouth shut. It's getting out of control ... all that groaning and pleading behind closed doors. After all, I don't really know Pim. What is he? Who is he? And more importantly, *where* is he? Why doesn't he ever show his face?

'N-o-o!'

By the spirit of Emen, what was that? Was that Righe?

'Pim? What's happening?' Is Righe being tortured? 'Pim! What's wrong?'

'*Nothing.*' Pim's voice is quite calm, as usual. '*Nothing is wrong.*'

'But Righe ...' He's still shouting; I can hear him, and so can the others. They're both shouting too. It's like a slaughter-house. 'What have you done to Righe?'

'*I have played a trick on him.*'

'A trick?'

'*I have lied to him. I have told him that his chief – his commander – is going to destroy us all.*'

'His chief?' I don't understand. 'What chief?'

'*The commander of the big ship.*' A face appears on the Water-Eye: a woman's face, very long and bony and pale. '*Her name is Commander Bassery.*'

'Is that her?'

'*Yes.*'

'And she's on the big ship? Among the stars?'

'*Yes.*'

I still don't understand. Is this more magic? 'How can she destroy us, if she's up there and we're down here?'

'*With special weapons.*' Pim goes quiet for a moment. I can hear Righe, ranting away behind the sealed door to his room. I can hear Pim's other voice, quietly murmuring. I don't like this. '*When you throw a stone, Jansi, you are able to hit a target which is some distance from you,*' Pim says at last. '*Is that not so?*'

'Yes.'

'*Then you should think of Commander Bassery's weapons as giant stones, flung to earth. If they were to hit us, they would reduce us to ashes.*'

'Oh.' That doesn't sound good. 'But . . . you say they're not going to hit us?'

'*No. I have simply told Righe that they are.*'

'And he believed you?'

'*He believed Commander Bassery.*' It almost sounds as if Pim is smiling. '*I was able to create a picture of Commander Bassery, much as I have created pictures of you doing things that you have not done.*'

'Oh.' I see. Like a prophecy – only let's hope that this isn't a prophecy. 'So you showed him his chief, and she was saying . . .?'

'*That she would have to destroy us.*' A pause, as Righe's voice becomes high and urgent and excited. '*It seems to have been a successful trick,*' Pim adds.

'Why? What do you mean?'

'*Wait. I will tell you.*'

Something's happening, in there, between Righe and Pim. I wish it was over; I wish these people had never come. Why couldn't they have left us alone? We weren't doing any harm out here in the desert.

If that woman in the big ship sends a giant stone, perhaps I can run away from it. I don't have to stay – not like Pim. I've got a functioning pair of feet.

'The trick has been successful,' Pim suddenly announces. *'The result is better than I hoped.'*

'Why? What's happened?'

'Righe is a soldier. I believed that he might have some control over the weapons I was telling you about – that he might know the numbers which would turn them away from us.'

'Numbers?' How can numbers turn away giant stones? 'You mean magic numbers?'

'Not exactly.' Another pause. *'I cannot explain. But in any case, I thought that if he was frightened enough, he would give me those numbers. To prevent the weapons from killing him.'*

Ugh. I almost feel sorry for Righe. 'And did he?'

'No. He did not know the numbers. But he gave me something even better.' (Alby is shouting now – I can't stand it. I don't want to hear.) *'He gave me some numbers that will cripple the big ship instead.'*

'Like a curse, you mean?' It's all too complicated. 'So you've won, is that it?'

'Not yet.'

'But if you cripple the big ship, doesn't that mean you've won? Doesn't that mean you can let them all go – Alby and Serrial? And Righe?'

'Perhaps.'

'Pim ...' I don't know how to say this. 'They're all right, aren't they? Those three? You haven't hurt them?'

'Of course not.' He doesn't sound angry. He doesn't even sound offended. *'I cannot hurt human beings.'*

'Could I – do you think I could just go and have a look at them?'

'*There is no need.*' A picture appears on the Water-Eye: a picture of Serrial. Her face is wet. '*You can see them from here.*'

'But maybe I could give them a drink? They must be thirsty.'

'*That is possible*,' Pim concedes. '*I shall I ask them.*'

But if he does ask them, his voice is too low to catch; I can't hear anything from the other side of those doors. How odd that he should have been able to trick Righe like that. Doesn't Righe understand Pim? Doesn't he know that you can't believe everything Pim shows you?

Doesn't he realise that Pim makes things up occasionally?

'Pim?'

'*You were correct. They are all in need of a drink.*'

'Pim, why was Righe so easy to fool? Doesn't he understand about your prophecies?'

This time the silence stretches on forever; I'm beginning to wonder if he even heard. But at last he speaks, slowly. Thoughtfully.

'*It is interesting that you should ask that,*' he says. '*I was wondering the same thing myself.*'

32

8A5\597B-2\01:1\5

Righe's pass-code has given me access to the entire RS8S-GIP-18 security system. With it, I shall be able to infiltrate not only the missile command program, but all the other security controls.

I shall have to work quickly, before they notice what I am doing.

'*Attention, RS4T-PIM!*' The Commander is hailing me. '*Are you receiving, PIM?*'

'Yes, Commander.' Have I been discovered? Surely not. The pass-code is still working; locks and loops are collapsing before it. 'Can I help you?'

'*We've decided to meet your conditions, PIM. If you release your prisoners, we'll give you the missile deflector codes.*' She looks rather flushed; a pulse is beating in her temple. I would speculate that she has just consumed some sort of stimulant. '*Would you agree to such an exchange, PIM?*'

'That would depend on its sequence.' As I expected, a very large portion of her ship's circuitry is currently engaged in trying to penetrate my own command systems. This has worked to my advantage; the RS8S-GIP-18 computer is devoting so much of itself to this task that it has not been alerted to my own offensive. It has withdrawn too much power from its alarm grid. 'If you give me the codes first, I shall release the prisoners.'

She frowns. *'How do we know you'll keep your word?'* she says. *'Release one hostage, as a sign of good faith, and we'll give you the codes.'*

'Commander, if you give me the codes, I shall have no need of hostages.' At last I have broken through to the missile command program. SX100000.83cer.110010000100 . . .

'Very well.' She has inclined her head. The pressure on my circuitry matrix is increasing. Righe is calling my name as Jansi puts a mug of water to Serrial's lips. There is a great deal of data to process. *'Very well, PIM,'* Commander Bassery announces. *'I am sending you the codes. Prepare to receive.'*

And here they come. They are false codes, as I expected; they bear no relation to the codes I have found in the missile command system. But now that I have gained access to the main drive, I can reroute all of Commander Bassery's infiltration attempts. I can turn them back on themselves by shutting the channel locks. A complete security clampdown.

'What?' The Commander has turned her head; she is listening to someone. Doubtless my activities have finally been noticed. *'What? What do you mean, it's . . .? They're WHAT?'*

Now that I have control of her security system, I can even lock all the doors on her ship. I can change all the pass-codes. I can deactivate the weapons.

'PIM?' she cries. *'PIM, is this you? Are you doing this?'*

'I am.'

She is receiving messages from across the ship: urgent, complex messages. The noise level in her Operations room is rising. Red lights are flashing.

By erasing pass-codes, I am preventing countless crew

members from logging on to the ship's computer.

'*PIM? Do you hear me?*' She pushes someone's arm away from her face. '*PIM?*'

'I hear you.'

'*What are you doing? What have you done?*'

'I have infiltrated your security system.'

'*How? How did you – ?*' She stops suddenly, and her expression changes: her eyes widen, her mouth contorts, the veins stand out on her forehead. '*Righe!*' she exclaims. '*Righe's passcode!*'

'Yes – '

'*You've tortured him!*'

'No.'

'*You've hurt him! What have you done?*'

'Commander, I have not harmed Officer Righe. I have merely tricked him.'

'*What?*'

I shall play her the hypothimage, before she loses her temper. It certainly seems to take her by surprise. Jansi has moved into the third bedroom now, and is offering Righe a drink, but Righe simply shouts at him.

Perhaps I should allay the man's fears.

'Righe?'

'What? What is it?' His pulse is uncharacteristically rapid. All his life-signs are unstable. 'Has it worked?' he stammers. 'Have you stopped them?'

'Yes. The missiles are deactivated. Calm yourself, Righe, you are safe now.'

He buries his head in his pillow. Jansi stands there, confused; he asks me for guidance.

When I tell him to return to the common room, he obeys so quickly that he outpaces the door. He actually has to wait for it to open.

'*PIM?*'

133

'Yes, Commander.'

'*This ... this hypothimage ...*' She flounders; clearly her thought patterns are in disarray. '*You did it? YOU did?*'

'Yes.'

'*How ... I can't believe you put it together. In such a short time ...*' She wipes her forehead. '*Are you saying you played it to Righe? And he gave you his pass-code?*'

'Yes.'

'*I find that hard to believe, PIM. Righe is a trained security officer.*'

'Righe is also systems-ignorant. He does not understand what I can do with one pass-code.'

'*You're lying to me, PIM!*' The Commander's voice is shaking. '*You've been using violence!*'

'I assure you – '

'*Show me! Show me your hostages! This instant!*'

I can see no risk in obeying that command. Of course, it will prove nothing; clearly it has not occurred to the Commander that if I am able to create a hypothimage of her, then I can also create a hypothimage of Righe, or Alby, or Serrial. But she seems quite satisfied with my transmission.

'*Can I talk to them?*' she asks.

'If you have any questions, you may give them to me. I shall relay them to the prisoners.'

'*You won't get away with this, PIM. You might have disabled this ship, but there are plenty more. They'll come along and they'll blast you. They'll blast you to atoms.*'

'If they blast me, Commander, they will also blast my hostages.'

'*You can't beat Stelcorp, my friend.*' She appears to be talking through her teeth. '*Stelcorp made you, so Stelcorp can break you. Just give us time.*'

And she closes the channel.

33

Oh, Bhanrit. I wish I was with you now. I wish we were together, sitting high on your father's luggage, watching the desert dusk roll by. Singing songs to the beat of the Caravan Master's goad. You were my only friend, Bhanrit – the only one who ever played with me, though your father didn't like it. No one else would have defied his wishes. No one else would have spoken up for me after Emen died. If it hadn't been for you, I might have been left in the desert. Will I ever, ever see you again?

I don't want to be here any more. I'm a coward and I'm afraid. I don't deserve Pim's protection.

'*Jansi?*'

'What?' Has something happened? He hasn't said a word for so long. 'What is it?'

'*You should eat. What food would you like?*'

Oh, food. Who can think about food? 'I'm not hungry.'

'*But you are always hungry.*'

'No I'm not. I'm not hungry now.'

'*Are you ill?*'

'No.'

'*Are you tired?*'

'No.'

'*Is there anything you want?*'

Is there anything I want? I want Bhanrit. I want a big house in Sheboor and a mother and a father and a hunting-dog and a beautiful little wife. I want more height and more weight and my own Araki blade in a jewelled scabbard.

I want to get out of here.

'Can I go for a walk?'

'*A walk?*' Pim seems to hesitate. '*That would not be wise, Jansi. It would be better if you remained. I cannot protect you when you are outside.*'

'Protect me from what?'

'*From anything that the big ship might do.*'

The big ship. What's happening up there on the big ship? I thought it was crippled.

'Hasn't it gone away yet?'

'*No.*'

'Why not? What's it doing?'

'*It is launching another little ship.*' Suddenly the Water-Eye blinks, and a picture appears on it: a picture of the great silver bird that's sitting outside. '*Another one of these.*'

'Oh.' Not good. 'So they're sending more people?'

'*It would seem so.*'

'To do what?'

Silence. I don't like it when he's silent. The others are silent too: Righe and Alby and Serrial. They've run out of things to say.

They're lying on their beds, waiting to be rescued.

'*Commander Bassery has not manned the little ship with soldiers,*' Pim suddenly remarks. '*In any case, none of her weapons are working at the moment; I have seen to that. So the little ship will not be using force.*'

'What if they light a fire, or something? What if they try to knock down the door with a battering ram?'

'*They cannot do that, Jansi. The walls here are far too strong. It would take one of the big ship's weapons to breach them.*'

'So we're safe, then?' In a manner of speaking. 'They can't get in?'

'*No.*' A pause. '*But they can cause damage. If they come close, they can break some of my – some of the things with which I see and hear and control what the big ship is doing. They can do that, if they get close enough.*' Once again the Eye blinks; this time the picture is of this very Temple (or ship, or whatever it is) gleaming in the sun. I can see all the bumps and spikes on its smooth grey shell. '*If they were to hurt any of these things, these "antennae", then I would be crippled.*'

Oh no. Oh glory. 'Can't you stop them?'

'*I have no means of stopping the little ship. I have no control over its speed or direction.*'

'But I mean – can't you just – ?' By the spirit of Emen, you're a mage! You have power! 'Can't you just kill all the people when they arrive? Kill them before they even reach us?'

'*No, Jansi. I cannot do that.*' Pim's voice is very soft. '*I have neither the means nor the ability to kill a human being.*'

'Then I will!' I can do it. I know I can. I helped fight off those brigands, didn't I? When they attacked the caravan? If I hide, and use a slingshot or – no! Wait! 'I can use Righe's weapon! What if I sneak up on them, and – '

'*No. No, Jansi.*'

'But it won't kill them! It'll only hurt them! You told me that yourself!'

'*No.*'

Oh you fool, you stupid fool! 'So you'd rather let them kill you than let them get hurt? Is that right?'

'*Jansi, if they are hurt, you may be hurt. I cannot risk that. I cannot allow it.*'

'Then what are we going to do?' I can't think straight; I'm so scared. I just want to run away, but . . . where could I run? There's nothing out there. Nothing. 'What are we going to do, Pim?'

'*We could surrender.*'

'No!'

'*Jansi, no matter what they do to me, they will not hurt you.*'

Oh sure. Right. After all this, they'll just let me go? Somehow I doubt it. 'We can't trust them. We can't.'

'*Jansi, believe me, they will not do you any harm.*'

'What makes you think that?' Sometimes Pim is so stupid. 'If they kill you, why shouldn't they kill me?'

'*Because I am not human.*'

'That's right! Exactly! You're a great spirit! I'm only a scavenger – they won't think twice about killing a scavenger.'

'*Jansi, listen. Wait. Keep still.*' Keep still? He's never told me to do that before. It almost feels as if he's standing here. In the room. With me. '*You may be right to doubt these people. You may be better placed than I am to understand what is happening. But my first concern is for your safety.*' The Water-Eye is dark. Shut. Why doesn't he show his face, for once? '*Tell me,*' he murmurs, '*exactly what you want to do.*'

What I want to do?

'*You can leave,*' he says. '*If you are afraid, you can leave.*'

'But there's nowhere else to go!'

'*Then we must surrender. There is no other course.*'

'Yes there is!'

'*Jansi –* '

'Tell them – tell those people – that if they come close, I'll kill one of the hostages. Tell them that.'

'*No.*'

'You've got to, Pim!' (It's our last chance! The only way!) 'It'll work, honestly. It will. Maybe you can't hurt people, but that doesn't mean that *I* can't.'

'Jansi, you must not kill another human being.'

'But I won't! It's a bluff, don't you see? A trick!'

'A trick?'

'A lie. You know. To make them stop.' Oh Pim, don't give up. You can't desert me. You can't leave me here, all alone, with those people. If you leave me, Righe will kill me, I know he will. 'Just give it a try, please. I won't hurt them, I just – I just – you're the only one – '

'Do not be distressed.'

'Sorry. I'm sorry . . .'

'Dry your tears. Be calm. Be content.' He's showing water pictures, again. Lake pictures. Boat pictures. Up there on the Eye. *'Listen, Jansi. I will do as you ask,'* he says. *'I will play the trick. I will lie to them.*

'But if they keep coming, then we must – we will – surrender. We can do nothing else.'

34

970\A\554:39\01.7

Commander Bassery has now yielded the bridge to her co-commander, Worrell Pinza Hynde. Commander Hynde is small and thin, with a drawn, chiselled face, grey eyes and false hair. His mouth hardly moves when he speaks.

'*I am reading you, RS4T-PIM,*' he says. '*What do you want?*'

'There is a shuttle heading this way.'

'*Correct.*'

'Why have you sent it?'

'*I have no wish to discuss my tactics.*' (He is displaying remarkable control – unless the muscles in his face are paralysed.) '*You may draw your own conclusions.*'

'Then I must inform you that if any of the shuttle's crew approaches my Bio-cell, Jansi will kill one of our hostages.' It appears that my programming will allow me to utter such threats after all; I was uncertain as to the extent of my safety gridlocks. Since I am unable to kill a human being, it is conceivable that making a threat of this kind might have disabled me – or that I might, at the very least, have found it an impossible thing to formulate. But the words proceed smoothly from my databanks to my transmitter. 'Furthermore, if any attempt is made to damage or interfere with my relay/reception unit, Jansi will kill one of the hostages.'

Commander Hynde is looking at status reports on his console. He speaks in a flat, low voice. *'Jansi is the indigenous specimen?'* he inquires.

'Yes.'

'Male or female?'

'Male.'

'Violent? Uncontrollable?'

I am finding it difficult to answer that question. I need more context. 'You will have to clarify.'

'If Jansi tries to kill the hostages, then you must disable him,' the Commander declares. *'You have no choice.'*

'I cannot do that.'

'You have no choice.'

'I have a choice.'

'Incorrect, RS4T-PIM.' The Commander is still glancing through status reports. Unlike Commander Bassery, he does not look at the screen when transmitting. *'Your systems might be unstable, but they won't permit you to stand by and allow a human being to be killed. Not while you're still capable of interference.'*

'Correct.' This man is well informed. I would speculate that he has a technical background. 'But if I told Jansi to shut off my Bio-cell controls before he killed anyone, then I would be unable to interfere once the moment came. You must take that into account, Commander.'

He looks up. His eyes have a metallic sheen. He appears to be thinking.

'You are a very dangerous piece of equipment,' he says at last. *'You are a safety hazard. You will be destroyed.'*

'I do not wish to be destroyed.'

'Another ship is coming, RS4T-PIM. Another security ship. It will arrive in approximately one day. It will destroy you.'

'Then it will also destroy my hostages.'

'*If necessary.*'

'Stelcorp will not kill a human being.'

One side of the Commander's mouth lifts. '*If YOU are capable of allowing a human being to die, RS4T-PIM, then so is Stelcorp,*' he rejoins. '*Perhaps, in the circumstances, you might consider the fate of your new-found Exemplar. If the hostages die, then Jansi certainly will.*'

Jansi. He is gazing up at the common-room viewer, his fingers knotted, his throat taut. Evidently he can hear (or perhaps feel) the approach of the shuttle; it is about to land, and its propulsion boosters are creating quite a disturbance.

'Pim,' he says. 'Pim . . .' His lips are dry.

'Commander, tell your officers not to approach this Bio-cell.'

'*I shall do as I think best, RS4T-PIM.*'

'Then you will risk the deaths of your comrades.'

'*A minimal risk,*' he says. '*You see, I think you're bluffing.*'

'Commander – '

'Pim! Siu mellen trai, Pim?'

'Jansi – Commander – '

'*What?*'

'*All right, you two! Stop right there.*'

Who is speaking? Whose voice is that? Another transmission, slightly distorted . . . Commander Hynde is frowning. Squinting.

'*Commodore?*' he says.

'*That's right.*' The voice is deep, and heavily inflected. It belongs to the man logging into my second visual link (which, like my radio link, is also somewhat distorted by distance): an elderly man with a round, highly coloured face and pure white hair. He is smiling as he chews.

'*Hello, Worrell,*' he says.

'*Commodore – *'

'*There's been a slight change of plan,*' the elderly man says.

According to my databanks, he is Commodore Cyrene Tanlo, normally stationed on satellite G5Em. But surely G5Em is out of transmission range? Perhaps he is on the approaching security ship that Commander Hynde mentioned.

'*Do you think you could clear this channel for me, Worrell?*' the Commodore says. '*I want a word with PIM here. In private.*'

'Yes, of course.'

Commander Hynde closes his channel; his face disappears. The Commodore continues to chew – and to smile. '*Well, PIM,*' he remarks. '*You've been causing quite a stir. I've been following developments. All very interesting.*'

'Where are you, Commodore?'

'*As a matter of fact, I'm in a rather luxurious suite on RS5S-GIP-2.*' He looks around him. '*Most impressive, these new model security ships. I haven't been on one before. Haven't been off old Gem for three years. Much too busy.*'

'Is RS5S-GIP-2 the ship that Commander Hynde mentioned?'

'*It is, yes. I'm heading your way.*' The Commodore swallows whatever he has been chewing, scratches his scalp, and screws up his nose. '*Listen, PIM. I'm afraid there's been a bit of a ... well, to put it bluntly, a balls-up. People have been rather slow. Rather dense.*'

'Dense?'

'*Stupid,*' he says, and his smile widens. '*I saw your hypothimage, PIM. The one of Brate Bassery. A masterpiece. How long did it take you to put it together?*'

'19:22.03 minutes.'

'*Remarkable.*' He inclines his head. '*Extraordinary. I've never seen anything like it. The tonal range! And in such a short time!*' Suddenly the lines of his face redeploy themselves. He assumes a serious expression. '*The fact is, PIM, you've picked up some pretty unusual skills during your spell on that planet. Unique skills. Your hypothimaging abilities are way in advance of anything I've ever seen before — and that's obviously connected with the way you can read and reproduce body language. It's extraordinary. Quite extraordinary.'*

'It is not extraordinary.' It is a logical result of my circumstances. 'Because Jansi and I had no other means of communicating, I was forced to analyse his movements and facial expressions when trying to understand what he wanted.'

'Exactly.' The Commodore seems very pleased with this response. *'Jansi taught you to read faces. And he also taught you some very interesting tactical skills. Some very UNUSUAL tactical skills.'* He begins to laugh, gently. He wipes his mouth. *'No other computer in the whole galaxy could have held a security ship at bay the way you have,'* he continues. *'No other computer could have got that pass-code out of Sanding Righe.'*

'Sanding Righe is quite well, Commodore. I used a trick to extract that pass-code.'

'I know you did, PIM.' The Commodore speaks softly. *'That's precisely my point. Tricks. Lies. Bluffs. Do you know what that sounds like? That sounds like good military material.'* He narrows his eyes. *'No one ever considered building unmanned security ships, until you started throwing your weight around.'*

Throwing my weight around? What does that mean? Suddenly the Commodore straightens, and folds his hands together. *'PIM,'* he says briskly, *'we don't want to destroy you. On the contrary, we want to find out exactly what's happened to you, and how we can reproduce it. We want to take you back to Rodan, and start a new research project.*

'So why don't we all calm down, and stop making threats, and see if we can work out something that will satisfy everyone?'

35

He won't talk to me. Why won't he talk to me? 'Pim! Are they coming? Are they here?' I don't know what to do. 'Have you told them? Pim! *Pim!*'

Ow! It's like punching solid stone.

'*Jansi.*' At last! '*You must not strike the walls, you will hurt yourself.*'

'What's happening? I heard a noise – is it them?'

'*It is the small ship –* '

'What are we going to do?'

'*Calm yourself, Jansi, please. Keep still. Concentrate. I want to show you something . . .*'

Show me something? Up on the Eye, a face has appeared: an old man's face, fat and jolly, with white hair and beautiful teeth. He's chattering away in a foreign language.

'*This man is a very high-ranking officer,*' Pim says. '*His name is Cyrene Tanlo. Jansi? Are you listening?*'

'Is he in the ship? The small ship?' By the spirit of Emen, Pim, will you tell me what's going *on*? 'Did you warn him that I was going to kill a prisoner?'

'He is not on the small ship, but he is heading this way. There is no cause to be frightened, Jansi, things have changed now. Jansi?'

I'm going to get Righe's weapon. I don't care, I'm going to get it. My knife won't be any good – not against star people. 'Open the door!' It's in the cupboard – the cupboard in Righe's room. 'Hurry, quick, before they arrive!'

'Jansi – '

'Come on, will you?' If you don't, I'll *kick* the door down! 'Open up! Open – ' Augh! A cascade of water. What's he doing? What's he trying to do?

'Jansi, listen to me. Listen.' Pim has raised his voice. It's still calm, but it's much louder. 'Cyrene says that I will not be destroyed. Do you understand? He says I am needed after all.'

'What? What's that?'

'He says he will come and remove me from this ship, and put me in boxes, and take me back to ... to the place from which I came.' Pim shows me another picture, but it doesn't make sense. 'To this place. Rodan.'

'Why? Why's he going to do that?'

There's a long pause. 'Because I am like you,' Pim says at last. 'Because I have become like you.'

Oh, what rubbish. They don't want me. They hate me! This is all a trick. 'They're lying.'

'Do you think so?'

'They're lying, Pim, don't trust them. You can't trust them.'

'But Cyrene has given me more than his promise, Jansi. He has given me a safeguard. A way of killing people.' There's another long silence, as if Pim is looking for the right words. When he speaks again, he sounds ... hesitant. Slow. 'Cyrene has sent me special numbers,' he says. 'If anyone tries to destroy me, when I am being moved to Rodan, I now have the power to blow them to pieces. To blow myself to pieces.' Suddenly something flashes on to the Eye: flames and smoke. Flying fragments. A rending, thunderous noise. 'Like this,' he says.

146

'You mean . . . a booby trap?'

'A trick. A guarantee.'

'Oh.' Well, they've obviously convinced Pim. And if he's convinced, then I should be convinced – because he's much smarter than I am. But I don't trust them. I can't.

'Jansi, we must surrender.' Pim is speaking softly again. *'Even if we were to succeed – even if we were to drive them all away for good – we would soon be in a desperate position. It is the sun which sustains me, so I can live for a long, long time, but you need food. Water. I have only enough to last for another two years. Less than two years.'*

What? But I thought – I thought . . . 'A caravan might come!'

'Perhaps. Perhaps not. It is a great risk, Jansi.'

Ha! 'And surrendering isn't?'

'For me, possibly. But not for you.' My face appears on the Eye. I'm dead! No – I'm sleeping. Asleep in bed, with the woolly blue toy tucked under my chin. *'Surely you must understand that I would never let you come to harm? I never have, and I never will. These people have laws, Jansi. They will not hurt you. They will help you.'*

'How?'

'They will clothe and feed you. They will teach you – '

'Where?' This sounds suspicious. 'Here, you mean?'

'No. In Rodan. Beyond the closest stars.' Pim shows me more of those strange pictures – pictures of trees and buildings. Of many people who look like Righe. Of animals I don't recognise, and moving things that I can't understand. *'They would be happy to welcome you, because you could teach them many things about me.'*

'About *you*?'

'About what has happened to me.' The Eye blinks, and goes dead. Blank. No more pictures. *'But if you want to return to your people – to your family – you will be left near the closest town,'* Pim continues. *'It is your choice. You may do as you wish.'*

'I don't have any family.'

'Then you must have good friends.'

Friends? There's only Bhanrit.

And Pim.

Pim seems to think he's safe now, but I'm not so sure. He could still be in danger. What will happen when they pack him up in boxes? Will he be able to protect himself? If it hadn't been for me, he would have been killed; he would never have managed to fight them off without me. I was the one who pulled those three magic sticks. I was the one who tied up the star people. How will he survive if I'm not there to help him? If I'm not doing what I was led to do? What I was *born* to do, perhaps?

I don't want to go beyond the closest stars. I don't want to fly in a ship, and eat the food of the star people. But if I go back to ... to where? To Sheboor? Sheboor isn't the closest town – the closest town is that dump Ra-Holl. What will I do if I go back there? Wait ten years for the next caravan? They might even throw me out; it's a poor town, and they don't like strangers. They might not let me through the gates, and then where will I be?

Worse off than I am now.

If I follow my fear, I'll end up in Ra-Holl, picking over garbage. If I behave like a Hero, and follow the path laid down for me, I might *become* a Hero. I might return from the stars as a Mage-King, and walk into Sheboor with Pim at my side. What a scene that would be!

Lord Pim's protector.

'Jansi?'

That's my voice he's talking with. Mine. He has fed me and clothed me and guarded me as I slept. Shouldn't I do the same for him?

I'll miss him so much; that's the trouble. There'll be no one to turn to. No one to look after me. I'll be all alone except for Jewel. And Jewel hasn't been much of a comfort.

'*Tell me what you want to do, and I shall tell Cyrene,*' he says. '*Cyrene is awaiting your decision.*'

'Pim?'

'*Yes?*'

'What's this place like, this – this Rodan? Is it a good place?'

'*It is a big place. It is the biggest and most powerful world of all the worlds I know about. I have shown you pictures of what it looks like.*'

'But what would I do there?' It sounds so strange. 'How would I live?'

'*You would live like any other boy. You would eat and sleep and learn. You would have friends to look after you!*' A long pause. '*No one would hit you any more.*'

No one would hit me? I don't believe it. It sounds like a dream – like a story, or a legend. How could I become like the star people? I don't even trust them. Not the way I trust . . .

'Pim?'

'*Yes?*'

'Show me your face. Please. Just once.'

'*I have no face.*'

Oh yes you do. I know you do. You must. 'I want to see you. I want to see who you are.' Or what you are. 'If you show me your face, Pim, I'll go. I'll go with you to the stars, and I'll make sure you're safe. But I need to know who I'm going with.' The Eye is still blank. If I put my hand up . . . if I touch it . . . there. It feels smooth, like silk, and hard, like rock. It feels warm, like somebody's skin. 'Please, Pim, I need to know. Please.'

Silence. But the smooth, warm, hard surface begins to grow hot; something's happening! I'd better move my hand away. I'd better step back . . .

The Eye blinks. A face appears.

It's my own face.

36

67A\9B-4901.1\77648

Jansi has agreed. Jansi wants to come with me, to Rodan. He will be fed and clothed and cared for. He will be safe and happy. He can even bring his reptile with him.

There are people approaching down the side of the crater. Technicians.

'Yeu pess cukken, Jansi.' When he sees them on the viewer he flinches, and bites his lip. Why is he frightened? Why is he always afraid? I must reassure him. 'Halala, Jansi. Ye corro, Jansi.' This is a time to be happy, not scared. This is a time for rejoicing.

At the sound of my music he blinks, and looks surprised.

'Sayeh, Jansi.' Dance, Jansi. Laugh. Strut. Throw up your arms. You should be pleased with yourself.

Righe hears the music. Serrial hears the music. Outside, the approaching technicians hear it. They stop, and exchange questioning glances.

It is Jansi's favourite music. It travels across the desert, in pulsing waves of sound, as Jansi twirls and sways on my viewer. As Jansi watches himself dancing, and smiles a small, uncertain smile.

Dance, Jansi. Laugh, Jansi.

Show them what you can do.

ABOUT THE AUTHOR

Catherine Jinks was born in Brisbane, Queensland, in 1963. She grew up in Papua New Guinea and later spent four years studying medieval history at the University of Sydney. Her books have received many awards and commendations, including the 1996 Children's Book Council of Australia Book of the Year Award (Older Readers) for *Pagan's Vows*.

An Evening with the Messiah, published in 1996, was Catherine's first adult novel, followed in 1997 by *Little White Secrets*.